To Jim, my court jester, minstrel,
and knight in hockey gear.
And to beautiful Beau, my fairy-tale ending.

Acknowledgments

Thanks to Peter, Carolyn, and Rick, three of the best writers I know. To Sarah, who backed me up, and Kathleen, who talked me down. To Sharon, Billy, and Mr. and Mrs. Fish, who let me hang around and made me feel like one of the fry.

I've always had my cards on the table, but I keep my friends up my sleeve. So I know where they are when I start to lose it. To my dad, the king of diamonds. My mom, the queen of hearts, and John, who is her king. To Al and Yas, my pair of aces. To Oma and Opa, who complete my full house. To Ken and Nora, who stack my deck. To Cathy the dealer, who forced me to play my hand, but dealt me a good one. To Kathy Lowinger, who invited me to the table, and Sue Tate, who taught me the rules. To my husband, Jim, the joker and my wild card, and to my daughter, Beau, who always makes me feel like a winner. And to Grandma Bennett and Grandma Homeniuk, who taught me not to quit when the chips are down. Without all of you, I wouldn't even be in the game.

PROLOGUE

What a Stupid Question!

"How do you feel about being here, Miss Black?"

It is my first day at "camp" and the counselor is taking an interest in me. How nice. Lets see, *how do I feel about being here?* Well, they have taken away my diet pills – nothing to tranquilize the wolf in my stomach. *How do I feel about that?* Next, during my stay here, I cannot partake of my favorite diet beverages. Too bad. A Diet Coke and a cigarette is the breakfast of champions. And, *how do I feel about no coffee for lunch and dinner?* The counselor looks at me with a pathetic pair of *how-do-you-feel-about-that* eyes.

"HOW DO I FEEL ABOUT THAT!!! *How do I feel about no diet pills, no Diet Coke, no coffee?* Let's you and me run down the 'happy' word list and see if any of them fit! *Do I feel glad?* Not a chance. *Do I feel excited?* Yeah, can't wait for the fun to begin. *How about joyous, joyful, blithe, merry, cheerful, contented, gay, blissful, or delighted?* Gee, none of these words seem adequate . . .

"Now let's try the 'unhappy' word list! *Do I feel mad-as-hell?* Bet your Red Cross! *Do I feel irritated?* Only enough to want to choke you! Yes, I feel indignant, resentful, irate, incensed, enraged, wrathful, wroth, infuriated, furious, nettled, galled, chafed, piqued, and really pissed off! Does that answer your bleeping stupid question?" I scream until my throat hurts. I scream loud enough to wake the dead and get the loonies all excited.

Apparently you can scream all you want at Camp Eat-a-Lot. I think if we renamed this place Camp Scream-All-You-Want, we would attract a lot more campers. *I feel great about the screaming part.*

Saturday

Clouds scream across the sky, turning the sun on and off like a lightbulb. Yellow. Gray. Yellow. Gray.

Turquoise ocean. Waves of melted glass capture the silhouette of a dolphin bodysurfing.

Sitting in Zack's car, watching the world through the windshield.

Be cool. Enjoy the view.

Zack touches my hand and releases the hounds. Hormones. Only the "hors" aren't "moaning." And they aren't just raging. They're breaking out of blood cells. Crashing through arterial walls. Bouncing off bone. My body a prison, with a riot going on inside. My mind the warden, trying to ignore the outbreak and assure the media that everything is under control. But Zack is a top investigator. He slides his hands up the back of my T-shirt. Finds the evidence he's looking for.

"Are you cold?" he says. "I'll warm you up." He pulls me across the seat. One hand under my arm and hot like

3

a branding iron on my ribs. Just below. The other hand he puts under the sweaty backs of my knees. His fingers feel like ice. Then Zack lifts me, like I weigh nothing, so I'm sitting sideways on his lap. It's a great position to watch the beautiful ocean ripple and surge and stroke the sand.

Zack's tongue and words drift in and out of my ear: "You're perfect. You know that? I love you. You know that?"

I don't know what to say. Don't want to say anything. Just want to be Said to. Done to.

"I think we should," he says.

"Should what?" I whisper.

A surfer with fuzzy cigar dreadlocks walks by and pounds his fist on the hood of the car and yells, "GET A ROOM!"

I almost go through the sunroof. He sees that he's scared me and his hands fly up in that *Stop! Don't jump!* pose, which causes him to drop his surfboard on the corner of the car. He picks up the board and searches it for dings. Zack is looking at him through the windshield like the guy is an idiot. The surfer sees the look in Zack's eyes and polishes the car where the board hit it. He gives us a Cheshire grin and a big thumbs-up. He turns, swings the tail of his board into the grill of the car, and charges down the beach and into the surf.

I thought Zack would be mad. He loves his car – just had it painted.

Zack says, laughing, "I think Einstein is right. We should get a room." He grabs me and kisses me. Hard. Runs his tongue along my teeth like you run a stick along a fence. Probes the back of my mouth. Finds my molars and sends an electric shock through me like he's stuck a fork in my filling.

The car is a greenhouse, all windows, and the sun pours in. Sweat on the glass and on the back of my neck and in the corners of Zack's eyes. Things sprouting with the heat. Fingers and tongues and nipples and I'm sitting right on top of that something that desperately wants to break through the fly of Zack's jeans.

I-love-you's rain down my neck.

"You're my angel; I love you here," he says, and pushes three fingertips into the skin underneath my shoulder blade wings. "You're my dolphin; I love you here," and he runs the heel of his hand along the inside of my thigh. "I really love you here," and he places his whole hand over the left side of my chest.

"You love my heart or my boob?"

"Both."

I want to open up his chest like a surgeon and climb inside, where it's warm and messy. "Tell me."

"I've loved you from the first time I saw you. At the football game. With the cast on your leg. I asked my buddy who you were and he said you were the girl who played football on the guys' team. And I've never seen anybody throw so many touchdowns standing behind the fence. You looked so miserable. But now I understand. You're not a watcher, Marty. You're a player. Let's play."

Zack is wrong. I am a watcher.

I had watched him that night. Like everyone else. When he left the alumni section of the bleachers and went to the snack bar for a drink, I watched the way the cheerleaders talked to him and tugged their hair. I saw the way Alan, the president of the spirit club, touched Zack's hand when he gave him his Coke and how Alan ran his fingertips along Zack's palm when he handed him his change. The way both the girls and the guys were jockeying for Zack's pole position. I had watched out of the corner of my eye as Beautiful Zack walked back and stood behind me. I ignored him, while everyone else around us tried to talk to him. When the game ended and even more people tried to get to him, I turned to leave; but someone was standing on my foot with the cast. I fell backward, and Zack caught me before I hit the ground. He scooped me up.

"Are you hurt?" he'd said. He looked scared.

I had a pain in my chest, but I said, "I'm alright."

"Want a ride home?" He smiled. Perfect teeth.

"Like this?"

"I could carry you, but then I'd have to come back for my car. Why don't we just make one smooth trip, okay?"

"Okay."

I watched how the crowd pressed out of our way. Looked at the snack bar and saw the lasers of hate shoot from the cheerleaders' eyes, and what looked like tears in Alan's. I blew them a little kiss. Those pom-pom girls who had refused to cheer for me when I made a good play on the field. They didn't like me playing with their boys, even though they thought I was gay. I did have something in common with Alan – I wanted to be carried off the field by Zack. I watched myself from above. Like a dream. And I couldn't believe what I was seeing. Me being carried from the football field by a guy.

"You remember that night when you carried me to your car?" I asked.

"Yes. You were my little damsel in distress."

"The last guy who tried to rescue me got bitten. During a game, a player from the other team stomped on the back of my knee and shredded it with his cleats because a girl had just brought down his quarterback. My coach ran onto the field and picked me up. Not hauled me up by the arm, like he did with the boys. He cradled me and started to walk off the field. All those people watching, congratulating themselves for being right. GIRLS SHOULDN'T PLAY FOOTBALL. The other team head-butting the guy who took me out. His coach even slapped him on the butt. I told my coach to put me down. He wouldn't listen, so I sank my teeth into his arm. And he dropped me. I limped off by myself."

Zack looks out his window. "I know. I was at that game. But I didn't know you were you. Never would have guessed that a defensive end would end up my girlfriend." He turns back to me and narrows his eyes, "Good thing we weren't going out then. I would have killed that guy. I'd kill anyone who hurt you."

"Would you?"

"With my own hands. I love you that much."

"Remember when we were outside the after-the-game party? The one we never went into? You asked me when I had to be home, and I said about two hours ago. You said you'd better get me home quick because you wouldn't want my mom hating my new boyfriend."

"I remember."

"Well, that's when I fell in love with you."

"So we've been in love for nine months. And I've hardly touched you. But God, I think about you all the time."

"I'm sorry." And I am. I'm also impressed. All Zack has to do is drive up and open his car door. Lots of warm bodies would gladly climb inside.

"I don't want you to be sorry. I want you to be glad you waited for me. For us. No one is ever going to love you more than I do. Make love with me, Marty." He gently closes my eyes with his fingertips. Takes my face in his hands and curls his fingers round the back of my neck and up into my hair. Brushes my lips with his and sighs.

"Don't." I didn't say "stop." I know the rules. Know I will blow this game wide open if I don't keep my legs together and the words "don't" and "stop" far apart.

"I know you're a virgin. I promise I won't hurt you."

"I know you won't. And I want to make love to you so bad, you don't know. But . . . I'm not a virgin."

"What?"

And I'd never told anyone. But now I could tell my worst secret to my best friend. I had saved something for him. The one I loved.

I open my eyes. Look into his. Assassin's eyes.

"He didn't hurt me," I say.

"You think I care about that?"

"What?"

"You lied to me. All this time."

"I've never lied to you."

"What about being a virgin?"

"I never said I was."

Zack shoves me to the passenger's seat. Ugly sucking sounds as we become unglued. He throws T words through the air between us:

"Tease.

"Tramp.

"Trinket.

"SluT."

I've heard all those words before. I hate T words. They're Torture. Look at ChrisT – they nailed him to a Tree. To a t. The word Trophy. But Zack doesn't have any with his name etched into a brass plate below someone else's. I look at the ocean, but it's turned on me too. Snarling. Showing its white teeth. Curling its lips back just before it bites down on the beach.

Zack gets out of the car. Looks at the front of it. Swears. Waves to the surfer and gives him the finger. Gets back in and drives me home.

As I'm getting out of the car, a couple more T words slide out of his mouth:

"LaTer, Thunder Thighs!"

I watch Zack drive away from me. At a hundred miles an hour.

The front door is unlocked. Open a crack.

Maybe . . . maybe . . . maybe not.

Mom is lying in her gutter of crushed velvet. The cushions have crusty spots from spilled rye and Cokes.

The armrests have Olympic symbols imprinted on them from too many forgotten, sweaty beer cans. Velvet is fragile.

I go to my room. It's a mess. She's been in here, tearing it apart looking for something.

I go to the kitchen and get every bottle of booze I can carry. Two in one hand, three in the other, and one under each arm. I go back to the living room.

"Wake up, Mom." I grind the words like meat through my vocal chords. Nothing. "WAKE UP!" She tries to open her eyes, but Smirnoff the sandman pulls them shut. I put the bottles down gently as if they are grenades. I haul her up to a sitting position. She slumps back down, but manages to prop herself back up with one elbow.

"You see this bottle, Mom?" I say, grabbing it from the table.

She looks, but can't focus. She clears her throat. "Where's Adonis? Outside? Ask him in to drink . . . to have a drink with me."

"You see it? This is you." I shake the bottle and drop it on the floor. It doesn't break. It bounces. She smiles. "You think that's funny? How about this!" I grab the bottle and smash it over the TV. That gets her attention. I grab the tequila and send Air Mexicana on a flight straight into the fireplace. *Crash and burn, worm.* She tries to say something. I don't care. This is not a conversation. It's a demonstration. But it's not enough. I want to break the world.

I go to my room and sit on my bed. Exhausted. Numb. The door creaks and Mom comes in. Kneels down in front of me. Head bowed, she starts crying. She looks so broken.

"I'm sorry, Marty. I'm so, so sorry. You're the best thing that ever happened to me. You're the only good thing in my life. And I keep screwing it up. I'm sorry." She's crying so hard, she can hardly get the words out.

I should hold her. Do something. But I can't. Can't tell the difference between love and hate. I think maybe both of those things go down so deep, they get lost in the darkness.

"I'm calling Dad. I'll go live with him. I don't care what you do anymore. You can drink yourself to death if you want to, but I'm not going to stick around and watch."

Mom draws into herself and carries herself out my door.

I call the operator in San Diego to get the number for Information in New York.

"There are three listings for Martin Black – what is the street address, please?"

"Can I have all the numbers?"

The operator disconnects and a robotic voice answers my question.

First number. Strike one. Second number. Strike two. Third number. *Please . . .*

"Hello?"

"Dad?"

"Marty?"

"Yeah . . . ah . . . I . . ."

"Has something happened?"

"Sort of."

"Are you alright?"

"Not really . . . I want to . . . I need to . . . can I come live with you?"

Silence.

"Did you just have a fight with your mother?"

"She's drinking. A lot."

"Well, I don't think it can be that bad or you would have said something before now. If you guys are fighting, don't think you can drag me into the middle of it. Look, I've got a contractor here. I've got to go."

Dial tone.

Mom comes back into my room. Holds me while I cry.

"I'm happy you're not leaving. Even if it isn't your choice. I'll get sober, Marty. I promise." Her words reek of guilt. But it's the last time they smell like gin.

That was the day Dad said no. Mom quit drinking. And I stopped eating.

Two Years Later . . .

DAY 1

JUNE 13

7:50 A.M.

First Morning

I wake up all alone in my "cabin." I don't care where the other girls are – I don't know them, and I'm not planning on staying long enough to get to know them.

Every time I closed my eyes last night, something would *beep* or *hiss* or *creak* or be announced or slammed. The white noise of the hospital prevented me from blacking out and the light from the hall blinded me.

I worm my way back under five blankets stolen from the supply closet. Maybe I could warm the room up by setting my bed on fire. Then the other "campers" could toast marshmallows (but not eat them), and I would be warm at last.

"Time to get up, Marty. Breakfast: five minutes." This voice comes out of the headboard on my bed. The mouth is somewhere around the corner, sitting behind a desk.

"SHOVE YOUR BREAKFAST AND THE TRAY IT CAME IN ON!" I yell through the layers.

"Nice attitude, Marty. Why don't you bring it to breakfast – down the hall to the dining room, last door on your left. Three minutes." The mouth has ears too.

I get out of my talking (and listening) bed and put on six hospital gowns. I alternate the openings. There are always bum-lookers in hospitals and I'm not going to be one of their victims. The gowns are all stamped PROPERTY OF SILVER LAKE. The staff will probably stamp me somewhere too, while I'm sleeping.

"Go back to your room and put some proper clothes on." The mouth has a face and a chest with the name NURSE BROWN pinned to it.

I check out the dress code. More than half the girls could be runway models. The latest haute couture consists entirely of baggy sweat suits. Black is big this year.

"You wanted me to come to breakfast and I came. Now you want me to go and put clothes on. I'm not naked and I'm not here to make a fashion statement, so what's your problem?"

"The point, not the problem, is that normal people wear proper clothes to breakfast."

"If I were *normal*, then I wouldn't be here. Here at Camp Eat-a-Lot, on Try-Not-to-Puke-It-Up Hill, in an institute called Silver Lake. I hear there is a private resort for nutbars, and a Club Med without the booze for alcoholics on the same floor. Sound normal to you?"

Nurse Brown burns to red. "You can change after breakfast," she says, "but from now on, hospital gowns are for weigh-ins only."

I turn away from the heat to check out the mess hall. The walls have posters of food tacked onto them. People smiling with perfect teeth at their perfect apples. Black type spouting nutritional facts. Not one piece of artwork has a calorie chart on it. There is no need. Anyone here can tell you the caloric value of an ounce of spit. Windows along one wall allow me to look at an outside world cut by little diamonds. I know the metal buried in the glass is for safety. I don't know who they are protecting – *me or the windows?* The table in the center is standard issue, metal and plastic, with fake wood on top that's never going to need polishing.

There seems to be some sort of seating arrangement. Team A on the left, Team B on the right. Anorexics and Bulimics. Eating disorder patients with order to their eating arrangements. Pickers on one side with too much food. Pukers on the other with not enough. I walk to the far end of the table and sit at the head. If they knew the truth, I could be drafted by either team.

"Marty. If you go across the hall to the nurses' station, you can pick up your breakfast tray," says Nurse Brown. She could have told me earlier, but I wasn't in position yet.

"When you go to hell, you won't need someone to tell you how to get there." *Check.*

Eight smiles spread around the table like cheering fans doing the wave.

"Start eating, girls," Nurse Brown says. The smiles fade.

Nurse Brown sits down at the other end. She clasps her fingers tightly in a church-and-steeple formation. And then tries to hide her religion under the table. She doesn't want me to see the white anger of her knuckles. She stares at me across the sea of food.

"What happens if I don't go get my tray?"

"We strongly encourage you to eat norm . . . solid food."

"And if I won't solidify?"

"You can consume your daily calorie prescription in liquid form."

"And what's my magic daily number?"

"Five thousand calories."

"You're NUTS! I'm not eating or drinking FIVE THOUSAND of anything!"

Nurse Brown's eyes tilt up at the corners.

"Then we will have to *tube* you."

I know what that is. I've seen them do it to a horse that went off his feed. The vet shoved a hose up the horse's nose, down his throat, and into his stomach. Then someone else poured gallons of slop into a funnel at the other end. And I watched the animal's gut slowly fill and bloat. The tube had blood on it when they pulled it out. The horse didn't like it. They sedated him.

"What 'we' thinks they're going to do that to me?" My hands start to shake, but I keep them on the table and my sights on Nurse Brown. She retreats to her natural state. Silent and patient.

"WHAT WE?"

The girls push back their chairs and swallow hard. One girl rubs the side of her nose.

"Actually, it's not a 'we.' It's a 'who.' And it's me." Nurse Brown smiles, revealing perfect teeth. *Checkmate. Shit.*

So That's How They Do It

The breakfast in front of me is only half of what I used to make myself after swim practice. But, that was forever ago.

I think this meal was made in that time period. And they are still going to make me eat it. Two slices of cold greasy toast, cut in half. One week's worth of bread at one meal. *Can't do anything about the butter.* Plastic astronaut packets of peanut butter and jam. *That's a double pass.* What looks to be six powdered eggs, probably from one cardboard chicken. I haven't eaten a real egg in two years. *I guess that record won't be broken.* Orange juice with a bendy straw. *I can handle that.* Maybe this place is a test kitchen for NASA. Except for one thing. There are no pigs in space. But on a scratched side plate lie five pieces of bacon. Real bacon. Real fat. And beside it, stamped with today's date, are two cartons of homo milk. Pig and cow stuff are impossible for astronauts. They're arsenic for anorexics.

I look around. Some of the girls are half finished. Some are already done. They're the bulimics. What they had to eat was nothing for them. One minute's worth of eating on the outside. But in here, here they are counting to ten or higher between bites. Now they are eyeing my tray.

"Eat your breakfast, dear," Nurse Brown says and lifts her mug.

Drink your tea. Bag.

Stop jousting and think. What's the plan? Eat this one meal. Get out of this room. Into the bathroom. Throw up their breakfast. Throw on my clothes. Call Mom. Tell her the doctor was wrong, she was right. She'll like that. She'll come get me. Take me back home. A couple thousand sit-ups, leg lifts, jumping jacks. Nothing but coffee for three days. Perfect.

I open both of the milks. Take a deep breath. Barely move my chest. *Control is key.* Half-piece at a time, I cram the toast in my mouth and sluice it down the shoot with one of the milks. One girl stares at me. With my spoon I shovel in the eggs, three loads, and chase them with the other milk. Another girl gives me the *why-are-you-here . . . you-don't-belong-here* look. *I don't,* I look back. "I'm going home," I want to say. I leave the bacon till last. That way it will be in my system the shortest time. And maybe the acid in the orange juice will eat away some of the fat. The pig on a plate is not so easy. I look around. All the anorexics save their bacon till last. The bulimics never had any. Just Special K and nonfat yogurt. I'd trade in a minute. So would the girl a couple trays away who is sawing her bacon into one hundred pieces. Twenty pieces a slice. I know why the plates are so scarred. She starts to eat the pork one one-hundredth at a time, using one point of her fork that she wipes after each crumb has left it and entered her mouth without touching her lips. She chews slowly. Ten times. Across the table from her, a bulimic has a death grip on her knife. And murder in her eyes. I don't want to be her next victim. I want to go home. *Follow the plan.*

With my fingers, I tear all five pieces of bacon in half. Take one-half of the pile and push it into my mouth. Big swig of orange juice. And I start to choke. Blow chunks of bacon halfway across the table, and OJ all the way out my nose. I finally stop coughing. I should have thought of this earlier. Nurse Brown is at my side with something bulging under her arm. I can't see, my eyes are watering so bad.

"Wipe yourself off and finish your bacon. Do that again and I'll place another order," she says, and drops a wad of paper towel in my lap.

I clean myself with the scratchy brown paper that is about as flexible and absorbent as concrete. Then eat my bacon, one piece at a time. And drink my juice. Through my straw. Slowly. *Done. Time to go home.*

I put my tray back in the slot that has my name in red marker on masking tape. I rip the tape off and start down the hall. Behind me I hear a tray get jammed into its slot on the cart hard enough to make it yelp.

"Where are you going?" A nameless voice.

"Disneyland." I keep walking.

"You can't go back to your room yet."

Five more steps till I can slam a door on that empty tray and nameless voice.

"They'll just come and get you."

Two more squares of blue-gray carpet to go.

"And *nobody* gets to leave that table until *all* of us have sat there for thirty minutes."

I stop at my door. Tilt my head back and talk at the ceiling tiles. "Why thirty minutes? Are we going swimming?"

"No . . . that's just how they do it."

Great. More rules someone forgot to tell me. Either that, or what goes on here is a national secret. I turn around. The shepherd's hook. She's gone. I walk back and sit in the chair closest to the door. The seat is warm. This had been Nurse Brown's chair.

Nurse Brown comes in, stops, wobbles, then walks to the far end of the table. She grabs the chair that used to be mine, scrapes it all the way back along the black-and-white squares of linoleum, positions it right beside me. This makes her closest to the door. In this weird chess game. I am now the pawn next to the tube queen.

"Trays back? Okay. Now that we are *all* here, I can start timing," Nurse Brown says and checks her watch.

Everyone checks their watch.

"Why don't we use this time to introduce ourselves and give Marty a chance to get to know us a little? I'll go first. I'm Celeste Brown, head nurse for this unit. I've been here at Silver Lake for nine years."

I'll bet eight of them were spent as a patient of the other units.

"You all know who Marty is, so we'll start to my left and go around." Nurse Brown turns her head and nods.

"My name is Nancy," the girl says and drops her eyes.

Then nothing. No "hi, Nancy" and a big wave from anybody. Even that wouldn't be as stupid as the silence.

"Okay, next?" Nurse Brown practices her lines.

"I'm Victoria, not Vicky," says not-Vicky, with the corpse-blue lipstick. And that starts the roll call.

"Elizabeth." Yellow eyes with black eye shadow on top and purple moons underneath.

"Rose." Saran Wrap skin around the bones of a carcass picked clean.

"Jamie." Blonde hair down to her waist, but half has gone down a drain.

"Bonnie." Pimples she picks at with blood red nails.

"Katherine. And this is Mrs. Burns. She doesn't talk. She's catatonic," says chatty Kathy, pointing to her left. There is more fat on a french fry than there is on Mrs. Burns.

After Mrs. Burns is me.

"Marty." *So stupid. They already know that.*

But Katherine. Katherine is the one who got me to come back. The voice that loves to answer questions that haven't been asked. *"That's just how they do it."* She wasn't reciting a rule, she was passing on inside information. On how they get you back to the table. On how they keep you from letting your breakfast join the rest of the sewage before it can be properly introduced. On how they torture you by making you sit. *I should have seen it coming and kept going. Too late. Plan B. I need a Plan B.*

"I don't feel well," I say to Nurse Brown.

"Just sit quietly. It will pass."

Hot under my arms and the backs of my knees. I never sweat. I'm always cold. *I must really be sick.* "I think I have a fever."

"It's just the food. Your body isn't used to it. Yet."

No way out. Just words. Just food. *"Yet. Just sit quietly."*

HOW? When I have to sit here while the waistband of my underwear becomes a cinch of razor blades slicing into my distended belly. And I feel I can't breathe 'cause all my lung space is being used by my stomach. And every nerve and fiber has a stopwatch that is counting the seconds that all that food has been inside me. *I must be gaining a pound a second. Thirty seconds – thirty pounds. Three hundred seconds – three hundred pounds.* And I'm going to explode. Every cell sucking back all those calories. Sweating. Celebrating. Doing what a *weak* body does best. And there is nothing I can do about it. I have no control. *I hate my body.* It was never my friend, but now it has buddied-up to the enemy.

This place is boot camp – with terrorists that make you do what they want by holding a tube to your nose. And they won't hurt any of the hostages if you'll just sit quietly.

Well, I know someone higher up. One phone call and this hostage is going home. Two minutes to freedom.

The Tank

Nurse Brown checks her watch. 8:50 A.M. "Okay, time's up. You've got ten minutes before GT starts; it's in the lounge today. You're free to go." She puts her hand on mine. The one I was using to push the chair away so I could get up. Away. *"You're free to go."* But the hand says *sit. Stay.* The girls silently stream around us and out the door.

Brown's hand is lukewarm and wet. I can't stand it and jerk my hand out from under her hold. "I need to use the phone."

"Marty, if you could just stay behind for one minute, I'll be right back."

"I have to call my mom."

"In a second, dear," Nurse Brown says and glides out into the hall.

I move slowly. *Don't make a sound. Get to the phone. Nine minutes to GT. Whatever that is. Probably Group Torture.* I turn and my knee bangs the chair and the chair scrapes the floor and Nurse Brown's tentacle slides itself around the door frame, feeling for the wall. Her cupped hand comes to rest. Let's me know my only escape is blocked. I sit. And wait.

If I were arrested, I'd get to make a call. I have committed all the crimes that got me here. They were perfect crimes in a perfect system that kept the world safe. I was the murderer. The victim. The judge. And the jury. I took care of everything. They have no right to keep me here. I have to make –

Nurse Brown's head swims back in the doorway. "Marty, you don't need to call your mom."

"Yes, I do. I told her I –"

"She'll be here in ten minutes. You can wait in your room," Nurse Brown says and disappears.

I remember now what a zookeeper said to me when I was little and didn't know anything and tried to stick my fingers into the fish tank. He laughed at me and said, "Oh, you don't want to be doin' that, honey. Octopuses are

23

smart, and they're good hunters . . . and they like to play with their food."

The Visit

"Hi, babydoll, how you doing?" Mom says and wipes the hair away from my face, but I'm sitting on my bed looking down, so the hair falls back. She tries again. Her hand, cold and smooth. Makes me shiver. She pulls away.

"I brought your schoolwork and I talked to Mr. Riada. He says whenever you get this done will be fine and not to worry about it being late, but I think the sooner you do it the better. Anything that needs to be typed, I can take to work and have Marjorie do it up. I can get books from the library if you need them."

"I won't need them."

"Marty, you have to finish these three papers."

"I'll finish them at home."

"You won't have time."

"Yes, I will. I won't go back on the swim team. I'll study instead."

"It doesn't matter. By the time you get out of here, school will be over. I know what you're asking, Marty. You can't come home. Just three papers and then you'll have your diploma."

"You mean, the real estate salesperson of the year and co-chair of the PTA can't have a daughter who is a high school dropout."

"No, I just think if you want to go somewhere . . ."

"I do. I want to go home."

"You said you wanted help . . ."

"This isn't what I meant."

"When you said to me that you wanted to see a psychiatrist, I thought it would be a waste of money. I was able to stop drinking. You could eat if you wanted to. But after you left his office, and I went in, he said you needed to be checked in to the hospital immediately. I told him it wasn't possible now; you had to finish school first, but he said, 'Dead girls don't graduate.' He said if I didn't admit you that, when you died of a heart attack or kidney failure, he would bring me up on charges of neglect. I don't know what you told him, but it's you who got you in here, not me. I'm in a corner, so now you've got to stay and do what they tell you and finish those three papers." Her voice is colder than the room.

"You're in a corner? Take a look around, Mom, while I try to get this straight. You want me to eat my brains out. *And* study my brains out. It would solve a lot of problems, wouldn't it, if I just BLEW my brains out!"

Mom looks at me hard, deciding how she's going to win this one. She can't. Her chin starts to go. Cue the water to the eyes. I can't watch.

I didn't tell that shrink anything. We sat for fifty-five minutes in total silence. Then he checked his watch and said, "Thank you for coming."

I look up. The tears have arrived onstage and Mom remembers her lines. "I can't do this today, Marty. Not today." And she leaves.

Well, at least you have a choice, Mom.

Mom is still here. The car and I are still stuck here. We both need her – if we want to leave. Things aren't going as planned. If they were, we'd all be halfway home by now, Mom on her second cigarette. Smoke filling the car. Fogging up the space between us.

I walk to the station to talk to the "guard."

"My mom hasn't left yet," I say to her. Her manicured nails and penciled eyes stay on the report in front of her. "I know my mom's still here. Her car's in the lot . . . can I see her?" The nurse looks up and stares at me like I just asked to see the queen. "Please?" I don't like asking for anything and they're already making me beg. "I need to tell her something."

"She's in a meeting, Marty."

Oh, God! She wants a drink. I made her want to drink.

"Can I go through there and find her?" I say, pointing to the obvious doors.

The nurse puts her work down. "Why would you go through there?"

"When they gave me the 'camp tour,' they said that was the ALCOHOL AND DRUG UNIT, so I'm assuming the AA meetings are in there – can I go?"

"You want to go to an AA meeting?" she replies and screws up her face.

She can't be a regular. They must have minimum IQ requirements for permanent staff. She has to be a temp from Idiots-are-us.

"No. I want to talk to my mom." *Here we go round the mulberry bush.*

"I told you, she's in a meeting."

Till early in the morning. "I know. She's in an AA meeting."

"Is that where she told you she was going?"

"NO! Can't you people say anything without a question mark?"

"Yes. And you don't have to yell. Your mother is in a meeting of a support group for parents dealing with children suffering from eating disorders. I won't interrupt them, but I can send a message downstairs. Do you still want to see her?"

She's not in the room with new drunks. Old drunks. The horror stories.

"Marty?"

"Ah, no . . . forget it." *Not today. She's safe for today.*

Go back to my room. To sit. And wait. *For what? For Mom to rescue me?* Too late. She's gone over to their side. *For Dad?* Fat chance.

Already feeling the fight leaving like fluid from an IV bag. *Drip . . . drip.* Something leaving. Something entering. *But what?*

The door to my room opens. *Mom?* No. Katherine. She is holding Mrs. Burns by the wrist. Leading her into my room. Mrs. Burns's fists are clenched into little bony balls – they unroll when Katherine places her on the bed, diagonally from me, and releases her grip. Katherine goes and sits on the other bed, across from mine. Mrs. Burns barely makes a dent on the bed, but Katherine makes her mattress work. The Marilyn Monroe type. Red lips. Big hips. She's twice the size of Mrs. Burns. *And so the welcome wagon arrives with her basket case.*

"I hear you like to punch windows. I don't like violence," Katherine says.

Jesus! What did they do – release an All Points Bulletin on me?

"Did your mom come?" Katherine changes the subject. Can't handle silence.

"Yeah."

"She gonna take you home?"

"How'd you know I asked her?" *Maybe this place is bugged.*

Katherine laughs and nods her head. "You think you're the only one to come here and want to leave?"

"No."

"One girl came in, and after breakfast her parents came and she threw a royal fit till they took her home. A week later they found 'her highness' hanging from the electric garage door opener. Neighbors found her 'cause the door was opening and closing. The swinging body kept setting off the sensor. She didn't kill all of herself. Just her brain."

More information than I need.

"They tell that story to all the parents. How come your dad didn't come?"

"Maybe you could interrogate me more later, but right now I'm not into it."

Katherine doesn't move. Doesn't get the hint.

"I'd really like to be alone."

"In here? Good luck!"

"Look, I don't want to be rude, but maybe you could take Mrs. Burns somewhere else and have a little chat with her. Thanks for stopping by."

Katherine laughs and puts her hands on her hips. "Is that what you think? We're just stopping by? We're your roommates, stupid."

Maybe they'll move me.

"You can ask to be moved but they'll just ask you a bunch of questions, not answer any of yours, and convince you to stick it out awhile – might as well get used to it. It's not so bad, you know."

"Neither is being brain-dead."

"Don't let them hear you talk like that!" Katherine's eyes get wide.

"Why?"

"They'll never leave you alone."

"They're not doing that now." My turn to laugh.

Katherine looks at me seriously and says, "Right now they're giving you a break – letting you settle in. Enjoy it."

Yeah, right! I'm settling up to my neck in quicksand while the natives stand around and watch. Only one speaks English. Says, "Figure it out, stop struggling. Think of it as a mud bath."

Strawberries and Scream

I put my tray down and sit at the end of the table. I want to be alone.

"I know it's a lot of food, but you can do it," Katherine says, and sits beside me.

"Thanks for your support," I reply. *Now go away.*

Fifth meal today. Dinner. Strawberries for dessert. These ones are washed and have the tops cut off. Not like the last ones I had . . .

. . . Three months ago. When I was still working part-time. Little deli that used to be called Full of Baloney. But no customers came, so the owner, Mrs. Van Daal, changed the name to the Phony Baloney. Served veggie dogs and tofu instead of beef tongue. Took down the salamis and hung up a HELP WANTED sign. She asked me one day when I was ordering my third coffee, "Vhat you sink bout vorking here?"

"I dunno?"

"Vood be good. I'm as big as house and you are like . . . like . . . *klein muisje.*"

"What's a kline mousha?"

"Means little mouse."

I didn't answer. I was thinking of us as Daal house and little mouse.

"You only one can fit behind counter vis me," she tried again.

"I dunno?" *Too much food. Too much.*

"All da free coffee you vant."

I hesitated. *I should be tough enough. Don't want to be weak.*

"Even ven not vorking!"

"Okay," I said. And so, between the counter and Mrs. Van Daal, I became the sandwich girl.

When I was working, she would talk about her customers. She thought all these people who ate health food were nuts. Was always trying to get me to eat the sausages she brought from home for her lunch. She liked things that were so well preserved, you could bury them. Dig them up in two thousand years. Get out your creamy mayonnaise, fresh bread, thick dripping slice of tomato; pile your stash on top and make a sandwich.

An older guy came in one day. Ordered tuna on pumpernickel. Sounded like he said "pumpherdickel." I had turned to make his sandwich and he said, "Nice buns."

"You want that on a bun?" I wasn't sure if I'd heard right.

"I'd rather have you on a bun." He leaned over the counter and smiled like a snake. Smelled the air with his tongue.

"Excuse ME?" I said real loud.

Mrs. Van Daal came barreling around the corner. Almost knocked me down. The cobra-man reared up.

"Vat you vant?" Mrs. Van Daal spat at him.

"She was helping –"

"I help you now. She is bisy. Liefje! Go to da back and get da quackamole. SEE? SHE IS BISY. YOU VANT SOMESING, YOU ASK ME!" And she never took her eyes off him.

I walked into the refrigerator. Soundproof, cold. Insulated from the world of people enjoying their lunch.

I found the avocado spread. As I peeled the plastic wrap off the little steel tub, my stomach roared. I could feel the acid drip down into my pit from the stalactites of my ribs. A cave so huge, hollow, and hungry. A black hole. Pulling. My hands gave in. My thumb tucked itself inside my palm. It didn't want to watch. Participate. Afraid to throw itself into the bowl. Hid just like it did every time the fist drove through window glass. Brave and crazy fingers formed themselves into a ladle. Dove into the mashed avocados. Smashed them into the entrance to the cave. All hell broke loose. The thumb decided if you can't beat 'em, join 'em. The closest things were strawberries and slices of Swiss cheese. Sucked into the vortex too. It all happened in about thirty seconds.

The compressor came on and made me jump, then the mind walked in like it was late for a meeting. After an explosion. Said, "WHAT THE HELL HAPPENED HERE?" Looked at the reflection of my face on the outside of the metal bowl, now empty. *Raped and pillaged.*

The mind was really pissed at what the hands had done. Shocked at the horror, but still taking pictures. Like a crime photographer. The evidence – red, green, and white. Question marks hung like meat hooks on my shoulders, pulling them down. What kind of anorexic was I? I had failed even at that. At any minute someone could have walked in and seen how I flunked the test. Working around food was a test and look what happened. *I can't do anything right. Can't even not eat right.*

Someone opened the fridge door. The first civilian on the scene. I still don't know who it was. I rushed past them. Out with the air from the walk-in. I kept going. One hand on my stomach, the other covering my mouth. Universal sign language for *I'm going to be sick*. Walked very fast past the bathrooms and out the back door. Scraped in behind the Dumpster. Threw up like one of those machines that kids squeeze play dough out of. On the pavement. Looked like a steaming, stinking mess of red blood, green guts, fragments of white bone. Something was pasted to my lip. I peeled off a strawberry leaf. I untied my apron and sanded my face with the starched white cloth. Put it in the Dumpster and covered it with garbage.

I walked home. The phone was ringing inside. I stayed outside my front door. Keys in my hand. The ringing wouldn't stop. I went in. Picked up the phone to make it stop crying.

"Hello."

"Leiveling, you . . . ?"

"Yes, I'm leaving."

"No leiveling, my dear, you . . . you make da most beautiful sandviches."

"Can't come back. I'm sick. Some sort of food allergy."

"Dat ugly man who vas here. You don't sink bout him. Okay?"

"I have to quit."

"I'll send you your check."

"No. Don't. Please. Keep it."

"My little mouse," I heard her say as I hung up. She was a nice lady. She didn't understand. Later I told Mom I'd been fired so she'd be so mad she wouldn't go in there.

Mom's words: "Fired again, Marty? I work hard, pay the bills, and you . . ."

I wanted to pay for what I'd done. Somehow I knew the check wasn't going to cover it.

"Hey!" Katherine raps on my tray with her fork. Brings me back. "At least eat your strawberries."

I'm paying for it now.

I'M PAYING FOR IT NOW. Screams only I can hear, in a voice locked behind a face like polished stainless steel. No one can ever know what goes on behind those things. My face and refrigerator doors.

DAY 13
JUNE 26

Lily tour

The clock on the dining room wall says we've been holding down our lunches for thirty minutes.

Dennis, who is usually the night nurse, comes back from the nurses' station across the hall. He looks at his watch. "Okay, girls, you've done your time. You have a half hour of free time before group. We're running it a little early today because we have a new girl in town. Her name is Lily. She's eight years old. And she's bunking with Victoria and Elizabeth."

The princesses don't look too thrilled.

"That's it for announcements," Dennis says and sticks his hands in his pockets.

We file out. Victoria and Elizabeth turn left and head for the walled garden. Katherine and I walk down the hall in the opposite direction. We have to pass Lily's room to get to ours. Katherine moves like she's on a mission.

I grab her arm. "I know you're really good at orientations, but I got this one, okay?" I say.

"Sure. Just don't scare the shit out of her," Katherine says smiling, pointing her finger in my face. "I'll be in the TV room with Mrs. Burns if you need backup." She turns and walks away.

When I knock on the door, Lily is sitting on the bed next to the window. She doesn't say anything. It hurts to look at her. I didn't know little kids could be anorexic. Eight years that looks like eighty. I'm guessing thirty-two pounds. It must have taken thousands of pounds of pressure to compress her into such a small package. I walk across the room and sit beside her.

Lily's mother comes in. Doesn't even acknowledge me. She starts skittering around like a squirrel, putting all of Lily's stuff away. She clutches a homemade quilt. "You'll need this, Lil, you know how cold it is in hospitals. I know best!"

Well, you oversized rodent, if you knew best, Lily wouldn't be here.

Her mom shoos us off the bed. I move to Victoria's bed in the corner and rearrange her stuffed dogs. Lily stands silent in the middle of the room. Her mom starts making the bed and going on about the quilt. Like Lily is going to argue and make her take it back.

The quilt is all in earth tones. The brown strangers in a white tundra. Patches of rocking horses, dolls, and the alphabet all stitched fish-line-snapping tight. No loose wiggling worm threads. It's a baby's blanket. But you would only notice if you looked real close.

Lily's mom finishes the bed, goes to Lily, and holds her by the shoulders. "Do what they tell you and everything will be fine," she says to the top of her daughter's head. She kisses it. "Lily's a very good girl," she says to me, and leaves.

Too good, I would bet.

Lily moves back to the bed. Sits on the edge. I join her and pick up a little bear that is wearing a yellow nightgown with the name BLOSSOM stitched onto it. I hold the bear by its back and sit it on my thigh. "Hi, Blossom, I'm Marty, how're you doing?" I bend the bear's head forward so she's staring at the furry paws in her lap. "It sucks being here, doesn't it, Blossom?" I nod the bear's head *yes*. "I know, but not all of the zookeepers are cranky, the water's pretty good, and you can have all the honey you want." I slowly raise the bear's head up so it's looking at me. "My room is right next door. Down the hall is the dining room. Every Sunday you circle what you want to eat for the whole week on your 'menu' card. Don't get the soup. I think it's made from dirty dishwater." I make the bear cover its mouth with its paws. "There's a TV room with cable and you can watch cartoons." Blossom raises her arms over her head. "Want to go for a tour and meet the other animals?" I lean the bear forward and make it look at Lily. "Do you want your friend Lily to come with us?" I throw the bear up and make it do a crazy dance in front of Lily's face. Lily smiles.

Welcome to the Group

I feel guilty. Lily follows me like a little cub as I take Blossom for a ride on my shoulders around the unit. And now I'm leading them right into a trap. Group therapy.

I walk into the GT room, but Lily hesitates at the door. She is smarter than the average bear.

"Come on in, Lily. I'm Rhonda, the group therapy leader. You can sit beside me for today," she says from across the room and pats the foldout chair next to her.

I put Blossom down on the seat and go sit on the other side of Rhonda because it's the only chair left. Lily walks around the circle of calm cool characters, slips through the small space between the designated chair and Katherine's, picks up the bear, and sits. Lily looks like a dwarf next to Rhonda.

Rhonda stretches out her long legs, slouches down in her chair, and crosses her arms. She tucks thick waves of her brown hair behind her ear. "Welcome to the group, Lily. We'll do the introductions in a minute, but let me tell you how this works. We do lots of different things in this room that give you a chance to express yourself, such as art and writing. But when we sit in a circle and talk, it's called group therapy. You can talk about your family, or you, or what's going on in the unit. There are only three rules: you don't have to talk if you don't want to; when responding to someone in group, we try to be kind and not critical; and what is said in here stays in here."

Except when it goes in our charts. So nobody actually says anything. If you keep your mouth shut, you can't hurt anybody. Words are like bullets . . . once they hit the target, you can't put them back in the gun.

Lily looks like she is sitting in front of a firing squad, Blossom gripped in her lap.

"Okay, guys. Why don't we start the introductions to Lily's left with Katherine," Rhonda says, as she claps her hands together.

Lily startles, but her eyes never leave the floor.

DAY 17
JUNE 30

Paper-thin Therapy

We are all seated like good little soldiers waiting for our next assignment. We never know if this will be the mission where one of us is captured and tortured. Where the enemy twists any information we give and uses it against the rest of us. The faces around the table show no fear. All of them would make good poker players.

The art therapist, who comes three times a week, walks into the dining room and says, "Today I want you to write about your neighborhood." She passes out thick yellow legal pads. Later she'll analyze them and try to squeeze juice from our paper lemons.

THE HOOD
by marty black

I had to move to a new neighborhood recently. My mom wanted me to finish high school at the old place, but my mom was told that if I didn't move I would die. A hundred-and-fifty-dollar-an-hour shrink told her that. Nobody asked me what I wanted or what I thought. I thought I'd rather die in my old hood than live in this new one. I wanted to kill that shrink.

My new neighborhood is bizarre. People are starving but there's lots to eat. It's full of drug addicts with nothing to shoot or pop. Plenty of alcoholics, but no liquor store for miles. The alchies go thirsty here. My neighbors are nuts. There's the guy who drools and pees himself. Every time we see him, we sing, "Plop plop, whiz whiz, there goes Jeeziz." Jesus and Mary live right around the corner from me – a couple doors down is Napoleon. Joan of Arc moved in last week and now we have to hide all our matches. She screams her head off every time someone lights a cigarette.

This neighborhood only has three blocks. On my block lives Catwoman. I call her Catwoman because she sits alone all day, just staring out the window. I think she would rather sit on the windowsill but the thick safety glass doesn't give her enough room. Instead she curls up in a corner. Her hair is falling out. I talk to her but she never talks back.

I had to move to another block for a day. One fun-filled all-expense-paid trip to the loony bin. The loony bin is on the wrong side of town. You have to watch your back in loonyland – not to mention your arms, legs, and butt. I'm not kidding. I learned the hard way that you should not leave your butt unwatched. One of the nutties must have thought I was fresh meat since I was new. He sank his rotten teeth into my fat ass. I should've seen it coming. Just before I got tasted, I heard singing behind me. "I see your hi-nee, it's very shi-nee, you better hiiide it before I biiite it." At least the attack got me out of the psycho ward.

It's hard to be normal here. Because if the neighbors don't make you crazy, "the watchers" will. Oh, the watchers are all very polite but they watch you all the time. They watch you sleep at night – they come right into your room and shine a flashlight into your face and on your chest to make sure you're still breathing. Sometimes I stay awake and wait for them. I hold my breath and when I can't hold it anymore, I yell BOO! They hate that. It scares the crap out of them. They scare the crap out of me, so I think it's only fair. It's annoying that they watch while you eat – every spoonful that makes it into your mouth is recorded. What's unbearable is that they insist on going to the bath-room with you and then they need to see what you've done, like you've just made them a present or something. Everyone who lives here has to . . . if they want to live at all.

Nobody in their right mind wants to live here. The funny thing is, this is where you are supposed to find your "right mind." And when you find it . . . that's when you get to live somewhere else.

DAY 19
JULY 2
10:19 A.M.

Therapy

We sit and stare at each other five times a week in this little office – the head-shrinker and I.

"What has four legs and chases cats?"

"I don't know, Marty?" Dr. Katz asks back.

"Mrs. Katz and her lawyer!"

"Why do you think that's funny?"

"Because it's a joke! Don't you think it's funny?"

"There *is* no Mrs. Katz."

"Never married?"

"Divorced."

Excellent. The guy who is supposed to help me can't even solve his own problems.

"Maybe you would like to talk about it?" I offer.

"No, thank you, Marty, I've already got my own therapist."

"Really?"

"Yes."

"No kidding?" And then I have to laugh. Katz will never be a kidder.

"Yes, Marty, I have a therapist I see once a week."

"To talk about your problems or your patients?"

"We are required to attend counseling."

"So we don't drive you nuts?"

"We listen to a lot of people's problems all day."

"I heard that psychiatrists have the highest rate of suicide in any profession."

"Who told you that?"

"You are being evasive, Dr. Katz."

"Alright, it is true."

"You guys must miss a lot of appointments." I look at my watch. Five minutes to go. I haven't bought myself enough time. I should have set my tongue to kill instead of stun. Too late, he is already recovering.

"Are you done, Marty?"

It's alive. "Yes, I think we're done. Not enough time to get into anything, so I'll just go back to my room now." I get up to go.

"Hang on, I want to give you something."

"It's unethical for a shrink to give gifts."

"Not a gift. A journal."

"For what?"

"If you are not going to talk to me, then maybe you'll talk to this." Dr. Katz he places the book on the desk and slides it toward me like a plate of liver. *Eat this. It's good for you.*

I stare at the book.

"Please, Marty. Tell it about you."

I pick it up. It's heavy, the cover black. I open it. White pages, no lines. "It's perfect. Black and white. My favorite colors."

"Someday you would make a good psychologist, Marty," Dr. Katz notes with a scrap of sarcasm. *There is hope for him yet.*

"Yeah. Maybe. Someday," I say, turning to leave.

As I close the door behind me, I hear him breathe, "If you live that long." Katz the no-kidder holds no such hope for me.

Journal Entry # 1

    I was given this journal / not-a-gift by Dr. Katz. He wants me to tell it about me. Okay, here goes.

    I am . . .

. . . that's my story and I'm sticking to it.

Sincerely, M.

DAY 25

JULY 8

Safe ~~Harbor~~

"Mail for you, Miss Black." The nurse slides the postcard to me across the counter like a bank robber passes a note to a teller. I tuck it under my sweatshirt and go to my room. Close the door and sit on my bed. Alone. The corners of the postcard poke at the butterflies in my belly.

Maybe it doesn't say anything. Don't look. Throw it out.

I feel under my shirt for the glossy side and pull it out picture up. Catalina Island. A bird's-eye view of Avalon Bay. One empty mooring is circled with the number 37 written beside it. More writing on the other side.

> Dear Marty,
> Zack told me you were there. I phoned your mom for the address. I would've called you but I don't know what to say. I'm still not crazy about what happened with you know who. But it was a long sail without you. And now that I know you can't be, I wish you were here. Love, Cherri
> P.S. Willy is driving me nuts! I hope that doesn't offend anybody. I hope they give this to you.

You know who. Paul. Cherri's then boyfriend. We were all at a party. Then Zack came. I hadn't seen him in a while. He saw me and started talking to Cherri. They were whispering. They left. And when it looked like they weren't coming back, Paul and I got together to commiserate. We had a few too many drinks. And then we stopped talking.

I haven't spoken to Cherri since. And now she's on Catalina Island.

Catalina Island. Cherri's words: "wish you were here." I'd have to walk twenty miles of San Diego freeway and swim eighty miles of ocean to get there.

I look at the clock – 11:43 A.M. Almost lunchtime for both of us. Cherri's reading some horror novel on the bow. Her mom is making ice tea and delicious abalone sandwiches down below. Cherri's dad will ring the lunch bell in a couple of minutes. If Willy isn't having any luck picking up girls on the beach, he'll zoom back to the boat in the Zodiac. Cherri will dive off the bow, swim to the stern, just miss getting hit by her brother, climb aboard, and start eating with her family while the sun dries her off.

I wish I was there too. In the cockpit with Cherri. For the sun and the sandwiches and the stars that we would sleep under. Every night they would watch over us as we settled into flannel sleeping bags, salty bathing suits for pajamas. The admiral would tuck us in and kiss us good night. The captain would make sure we understood we didn't have authorized shore leave. It was always the middle of the night before Willy made it home. He would knock on the hull for me to give him the "all clear."

Three taps on the door make me jump. I fling the postcard at the trash beside my bed, but it lands short.

Katherine slinks into the room. "I didn't mean to startle you."

"Why do you knock on the door to your own room?"

"Just habit." She looks down at the postcard.

"You do that at your own house?"

"Yeah. My father is a producer in Hollywood. Ever since my mother left, I never know what I'm going to find behind a door . . . I was surprised when I saw you behind this one. You look so different when you smile."

I pull everything on my face up.

"Never mind . . . Nurse Brown says lunch is in five minutes." Katherine rolls her eyes and leaves.

I lean over and pick up Cherri's postcard. The quarter-moon slice of beach at the bottom of Avalon Bay looks back at me. I hide the smile under my pillow.

DAY 27
JULY 10

"Family Session"

Jackie comes in my room and sits beside me on the bed.

"So your dad is coming today," she says, casting for a pretherapy bite.

"Yes. My father is supposed to come," I reply and walk away, letting her know the fish isn't hungry.

"Your mom called and wants to join us."

"NO!" It just comes out.

"Not ready?"

"I don't remember being a nuclear family. Only the fallout." *It won't go well. She'll drink. And it'll be my fault.*

"Okay."

"I just want to see my dad."

Jackie nods *yes* like I just took a test and got the grade she expected. I actually like Jackie, even though she is one of the enemy. She doesn't take or catch shit from anybody;

it just bounces off her. She's shorter and a lot rounder than all of us. That's what's funny. You can be the one looking down at her and find yourself intimidated. Jackie really cares. She comes in your room, throws her rump up onto your bed, and gives you a big squeeze – whether you like it or not. It doesn't matter to her what you like. It matters to her what you need. Jackie thinks my father and I need to have a "family session" with her. I was going to tell Jackie that my father doesn't need anything (or anyone), but I don't. I think it might be more interesting to let Jackie find that out for herself. Besides, I'm going to have the best seat in the house and for once it won't be the hot one.

Jackie's office isn't on this floor. It's somewhere down in the basement of the institute. I remember reading an article about electric chairs in prisons. They are always in the basement. When you have a "family session" with Jackie, you have to wait in your room until a nurse comes to get you. The escort of the day knocks gently at your door and tells you it's time. Walking down the hall, it's hard not to notice the salute of silence. No one ever comes back from Jackie's office the same as they went in. There was one girl who never came back at all.

Today is to be double treat day. I have to go to art therapy before the meeting with my father. While everyone is carving into their paper with the ever-popular black Crayola, I decide to go with every color but. The crassly named crayons are brand-new. Never used but probably years old. The art therapist must have to call the manufacturer and special order cases of all-black crayons.

I watch the art therapist pretend not to be watching me. When I pick turquoise blue to draw the sea, she holds her breath. I use blue-green and teal blue to draw the depths, and her eye starts to wink all on its own. Her hands start quivering when thistle and cornflower shade in hulls of tall ships, reflecting a sunrise. When mahogany and bittersweet make masts for giant sails of salmon and apricot, she has to go get coffee. I wax the sunrise daffodil and periwinkle and she damn near passes out. I think the possibility of going into the staff lounge and announcing her incredible breakthrough is just too much.

I'm not quite finished when a loud knock comes at the door.

It's Jackie. She's here for me. The only sound now is the clawing of my chair. It's too early. Or maybe my father is early. *That's a first.*

"Marty?" Jackie calls, even though I am already out of my seat.

We walk toward the elevator and then wait forever.

"What, Jack, no last meal or rites?"

"Since you're an anorexic and an atheist, I thought we'd skip them."

"Thank God you have a sense of humor, Jack, 'cause you're going to need it with my dad."

As the elevator to the basement finally opens, I hear Jackie mutter "no kidding."

We get to Jackie's office and she opens it with a key.

"Did you lock my dad in so the loonies won't get him?"

When she opens the door to the dreaded office, there is nothing inside except a desk. No whips or chains or electrical contraptions. No plants or pictures. Jackie opens a closet that she pulls only two chairs out of. Then I realize that unless she is going to pull my dad out of the closet, there is no father either. Jackie points to one of the chairs and gives me a stern *sit* with her eyes.

"Your father isn't coming," she says. Jackie isn't stupid enough to say, so how do you feel about that?

"Well, Jackie, my father not showing up for our big FAMILY SESSION – that's a FUCKIN' SURPRISE."

Jackie doesn't offer an explanation. She knows I'm not in a place to hear one. The silence hurts. I start to make a joke and cough. Then I cry.

DAY 28
JULY 11

Day After

Twenty-six hours since my father pulled a no-show. Twenty-five hours since I left Jackie's office. Twenty-four hours since my *Tall Ships at Sunrise* suffered a total eclipse of black wax.

I'm sitting in the lounge, counting the hours that have passed since certain events in my pathetic life have elapsed.

"Marty, it's your dad on the phone – wanna talk to him?" Lily squeaks, peaking from behind the doorjamb.

I want to say no. I want her to tell him I said, "Go to hell – straight to hell, do not pass GO and collect $200.00, just go to hell." But I don't. The only time I say no to my father is when he asks me if I want something to eat. And every time I step on the scale and another pound evaporates, I say go to hell.

I look up to ask Lily to tell him I'm coming, but she has disappeared. I know she is still there, just around the corner.

"I'll be there in a minute. Don't worry, Lily, I don't shoot the messenger . . . unless they deserve it." I hear Lily take off down the hall as fast as two toothpicks can go.

I leave the lounge and pick up the receiver on the wall.

"Hi." *One hollow dam of a word.*

"Hello, Marty, how are you?"

"Fine." *Control the flow.*

"What's wrong?"

"Nothing." *Check the cracks, the pressure, just a little longer.*

"Look, Marty, I couldn't make it yesterday. The meeting in LA ran over and I didn't get back to New York till after midnight, so it was too late to call."

Dad's dam is starting to falter. I want to say if he had time to call Jackie, why not me? "Okay."

"Okay, what?"

"Just okay, alright, whatever." *Too many words, too much tone, the needles are heading for red.*

"What do you want from me?"

You don't have enough time. I'll send you the books – one, two, and three – when I've written them. "Nothing." *Code word for "everything."*

"It doesn't sound like that. I'm trying. I'm not only trying, but I'm paying $1500.00 a day for them to fix you and you don't seem to be trying! You didn't even write three simple essays."

Oh, I'm trying alright. Just ask the art therapist, who is probably still flying down the Pacific freeway or wrapped around some pole. Lucky bitch.

"Did you hear me, Marty? $1500.00 a day. Do you know how much that adds up to?"

I want to say, "Yes, Martin. I was 87 pounds when I came in. In four weeks (twenty-eight days), I've gained exactly two pounds. The cost, including Dr. Katz's useless fifteen minute visits five times a week, and the family session you didn't show for, makes a grand total to date of $47,400.00. I'm worth $533.00 a pound. That makes me the most expensive meat in town." I want to tell him I calculate each day how much I cost him, just in case there is a pop quiz. All I say is, "A lot."

"You have no idea."

"I'm sorry, Dad – I'll try harder."

"You do that. And I'll talk to you next week."

Yeah, Martin, I'll talk to you in $11,850.00.

"Lily"

I can't believe it happened again. I'm the one who gets hurt, and it's me who ends up apologizing. My feelings are always my fault. A fault the size of the San Andreas that no one seems to see. There are huge, gaping canyons underneath the ocean. Nobody sees them either.

I don't feel like diving any deeper into my psychiatric rift. I might get the bends. I decide to go find Lily and make sure I haven't traumatized her.

Lily is burrowed under her quilt, curled in a little ball. I can't help thinking of her as a little Lily bulb in a flower bed. A lily that will never push its nose up and see the sun if it doesn't get something to eat. *This Lily is more likely to be pushing up daisies.* Bulbs can still be alive, even if they look dead. Brown and shriveled, waiting for someone to give them a chance to grow up.

"Come on out, Lily," I say, more to myself than to the bulb.

No answer from the bed.

"Lily, it's Marty." *Like she doesn't know who it is.*

"Hi." *A crack, somewhere to start.*

"Are you okay?" I hate the word "okay" because compared to somebody in the world, everyone is "okay."

"Yes," says Lily.

"I didn't mean to scare you earlier. I'm sorry." *See Dad, it's not so hard to say you're sorry when you screw up.*

"Uh-huh."

"Lily, I said I'm sorry. Now come out from under there and talk to me!" My pitch rises like a wave. I catch both of us by surprise. "I'm sorry." I pull back the quilt.

"You said that." Lily blinks back.

"No. Now I'm sorry for raising my voice."

"It's okay."

"No, it's not, Lily. I hate when my father does to me what I just did to you. And you shouldn't take it."

"Look who's talking." Lily sits up and smiles. A little kid smile.

I take her face in my hands and kiss her forehead. But, I find that I can't let go. I can't remember the last time I hugged someone, or someone hugged me. I think Lily has the same problem. After a few awkward attempts, I put her arms around my waist; she drops her head into my shoulder and I pull the quilt around both of us. It is the warmest I have been. Ever.

I look up to see Dennis standing where I had started. He is wiping spilled coffee from his Rolling Stones T-shirt. Dennis is usually the face and flashlight I yell BOO at, at three o'clock in the morning. I call him Dennis the menace. Someone has to speak or Dennis's eyeballs are going to dry out.

"Dennis, can I help you?" Second stunner in a row. Usually my greeting to Dennis consists of "piss off."

Dennis finally blinks and clucks, "Lunch, girls."

Lily unwraps her tendrils from around their stake.

"Come on, Lilybud, time for some fertilizer."

"I don't think it tastes that bad."

I laugh, and Lily, the little girl, smiles.

DAY 32

Field Trip

"After group, you need to go right to your rooms and get ready for an outing. We'll meet by the south doors at 2:20. A new nurse will be accompanying us. His name is Carrey. Anybody have anything else?"

I raise my hand. Stretch it up high. I can see Rhonda visibly flinch.

"Yes, Marty," Rhonda sighs.

"I really wanted to tell the group what's been bothering me. Really try and work through all that pent-up anger with the support of my peers. But I guess we have to go on this field trip, so maybe next time." I give Rhonda my most understanding smile.

"Yes. Next time I will call on you first. Yes, Lily," Rhonda says, dismissing me and looking hopefully at Lily.

"Are . . . are the *others* going too?" Lily asks, while trying to shred her cuticles with her teeth. Normally she is a vegetarian except when the subject of the *others* comes up.

"Yes, Lily, they are, but I've worked here seven years and nothing has ever happened."

"Okay," Lily replies and becomes a cannibal.

"Any more questions? Answers? Alright, girls, go get ready," Rhonda says, and gives one sharp clap like she'd just called a play and is breaking up the huddle.

On the Bus

We pile on the bus in our sweatshirts and jeans. The *others* are already on, sweating in their shorts and T-shirts. I herd Lily into the seat between me and the window. Make her sit on her hands. Tell her there is actually a lot of calories and a fair amount of cholesterol in human skin. She stops her finger feast.

The loonies are up front in case someone freaks out. The druggies in the back so they won't try to escape. And us in the middle.

The druggies are kicking the backs of seats. Picking lint off their cushions. Tapping the metal around the tinted glass of the windows – windows that won't open. They try to open their windows. They look trapped behind the bright whites of their eyes. The loonies are sitting cross-legged like they're on someone's sofa. Just visiting. Enjoying the atmosphere, their eyes glazed over like they got lost in the middle of a conversation. It's not right. The loonies should be losing it, but they can't 'cause they're on drugs. And the druggies should be out of it, but they're not because their drugs have been taken away. . . . I wonder if they ever look at each other and say to themselves, "I remember what it was like to be you."

First Stop – Seaport Village

I call this place Surreal Village. A Camelot where tourists and their gold cards can safely float around in their vacation bubbles and pretend that the real world doesn't exist. No mess. I have been here before with my mother. This is one of her favorite places.

It's perfect for the *others*. No clowns or homeless people to scare the loonies or to give the druggies flashbacks. Only coffee mugs with stupid cartoons and I HEART THIS and I HEART THAT.

After they unload the *others*, we remain.

For the first time I notice the new nurse. He's sitting at the front of the bus. I had thought he was one of the mental patients.

Our Stop — The Track

"What color car are you going to take?" Lily asks me.

"I don't know, Lil, black I guess."

"I want a pink one," Lily says.

I take one ride around the track and then get waved to the shoulder by Rhonda. I had tried to run Carrey-the-new-nurse off the track and up into the tires. I gave him a *you're welcome* finger as I passed his red car. I guessed from Rhonda's urgent need to see me that I was busted.

"What are you trying to do, Marty?"

"Uh . . . I'll give you a hint. Run him off the road."

"Why?"

"I don't like him."

"Why?"

"Look at him. Driving around like he's King Shit!"

"That's it? The way he's driving?"

"No. Look at his jeans. I bet they don't come in sizes; they come in spray cans. And I'm pretty sure that there aren't many left of what died to make those boots. He's disgusting."

"Oh, Marty," Rhonda says, her shoulders caving.

We both watch the rest of the girls for a while. Most have removed their sweatshirts. Sitting in those cars when they are coming right at you, you can only see their helmets and their hands. And their smiles. They look normal for just a couple of seconds. Until they turn the corner and you see them from the side. T-shirt sleeves flapping like check-ered flags. Then you notice their impossibly thin arms. Little pipe cleaners bent in a V, driving a car.

"I'm going to wave them in. You wait here," Rhonda says, getting off the hood of my car.

"Wait. Just let them go round one more time . . . please."

Old MacDonald Had a Farm

Next stop, ice cream. Carrey's walking ahead like he's leading us to water. Rhonda's in the rear, herding us like a Border collie.

"*Shee awww. Shee awww.*" I do my best donkey imita-tion and Rhonda looks at me. Raises the left eyebrow. The eyebrow that says *don't be an ass*. I obey and *moo* back at her.

It catches on.

"*Oink, oink!*" pigs Rose.

"*Baa, baaa!*" sheeps Nancy.

"*Honk, honk!*" gooses Katherine.

"*Mhaa, mhaa!*" goats Jamie.

"*Baaawcck, bock, bock, BAAAWCK!*" chickens not-Vicky and Elizabeth – queens of the coop.

Bonnie makes the sound of an animal that no one can figure out. But it is obvious the poor thing is in the middle of being slaughtered.

Catwoman does nothing but pad silently along.

Lily tugs at my sweatshirt. I look down. She is concentrating very hard on twitching her nose.

"What are you doing?" I ask.

"I'm being a bunny," Lily replies.

Of course. Something that has to chew, or it will die. A voiceless, defenseless creature.

"That's enough!" barks Rhonda.

The Trough

Definition of ridiculous. Ten eating disorder inmates at a public snack bar. The real reason. The whole reason for this expedition into the outside world. To get us to eat on the outside. And you would think we would appreciate the change of menu. Anything has got to be better than the mystery-meat lasagna and ralphabet soup they make us shove down our throats.

"Okay, girls, who's first?" Carrey says, a little too loud.

Silence.

"Why don't you go? You're at the front of the line. Or are you watching your figure?" I inquire.

"No. I'm just not hungry," he answers.

We all wheel around to check Rhonda's browometer. The left one is on the rise and pointing in Carrey's direction. He doesn't notice. He scans his little harem. Carrey's eyes rest on Lily.

"I'll go!" I say, and place Lily behind Nancy. I walk to the order window. "I'll have a medium soft chocolate ice cream, with chocolate syrup on top and Reese's Pieces layered in a cup. No cone. Please." Carrey smiles. Solved all my problems with an edible oil product. Snack bar Sally (that's what it says on her name tag) hands me my prize for going first.

"Now here's an example of someone who is trying," Carrey announces. I have the first spoonful halfway to my mouth. Beyond the spoon, I see a little boy at the end of the line. Either he's overexcited about getting a treat, or he really has to go pee. Or both. I decide to solve one of his problems.

"Here you go, kid. Enjoy all five hundred and twelve calories," I say, squatting down so I can smile in his eyes and hand him the cup. His bodyquaking stops. He accepts my offering in silence.

I march back to Carrey. "I believe that is an example of someone who is trying," I tell him. Katherine giggles.

"You are very naughty, Marty," he scolds.

"Naughty? Oh, of course. I've been a bad girl, very bad. You're right. Oh, *pleeease*, Carrey. Straighten me out. With your boots. Kick me, beat me, make me eat Hagan Daaz!" I fall to my knees and beg. Hands together, eyes closed. A soft tap at my shoulder. I open my eyes. Carrey is looking down at me, arms folded. Then he directs his gaze to my side. I turn my head. It's my little Lancelot. He speaks.

"My mom says I can't take stuff from strangers. Even ice cream."

The Summons

"Carrey wants to see you in the psych office," Nancy says, walking past my door in the opposite direction of the little hole we have to meet our shrinks in. When they come.

The door is closed when I get there. I have to knock for permission to enter somewhere I don't want to go.

"Come in. Yes, Marty, sit down," Carrey says, offering me the chair in front of the desk.

I sit. The room is closet sized, but feels even smaller today.

"Oh, could you close the door?" he asks. Commands.

I stand. Close the door.

Please, sit down, he gestures.

I sit. Again.

"Well," he says.

"Well, what?"

"Do you know why you are here?" he says, putting his elbows on the desk and rubbing his hands together.

More stupid questions. "Only the gods know that," I say, looking up at the ceiling.

"Okay. Do you have an idea why *I'm* here?"

"You are the nephew of someone on the board of directors. You couldn't get a job on your own. They felt sorry for you and put you here?"

"Very clever, Marty. I assure you I have a degree and am no relation to anyone on the board."

"Then you must be sleeping with one of them."

"Actually, it's these types of statements you make that prompted me to speak to you alone."

"Then what can I do for you, Carrey?"

"You see, that's just it," he says, polishing the toe of his boot with his thumb. "Your interest in doing for, or perhaps with, me."

"Excuse me?" *What the hell is he talking about?*

Carrey gets up and sits on the corner of the desk in front of me. Leans down into my face. "Marty, I'm concerned that you have a desire for a relationship with me that, although it is natural, is inappropriate at this time and probably unlikely in the future."

Oh, my God. Think think think. "You must have gotten high marks in school," I say.

"I was fourth in my class." He smiles.

"I'm surprised you weren't first. Your ability to see right through me like that. I do have a special thing for you. Even though we've only been together one afternoon, I'll admit, I would like to do inappropriate and probably unnatural things *to you.* And you know what? I really don't feel as if I'm in control of myself, being in the same room with you. So I think I should leave."

"That's fine for now, Marty, but I think we should talk about this again as soon as possible. They are giving me my own office tomorrow. You can come and see me privately any time you like. I would like to help. You don't have to talk to anyone about this. I'll be on rotation here for six weeks."

"I really should go now. I don't trust myself. You understand."

"I do, Marty, and I'll see you soon I hope."

"Good-bye, Richard."

"It's Carrey," he says, looking at me and sort of laughing.

"You still don't get it, do you . . . SAY GOOD NIGHT, DICK!"

The Cow

I want to run, but not away. Run to Dennis. I make myself walk to the nurses' station. I can see Dennis on duty now, but he doesn't see me until I walk behind the big desk, past him, and into the meds room. I know he has to follow me. No patients allowed in the meds room. He comes in. I shut the door. He waits while I massage my hands. Try to breathe my heart rate into something less than a gerbil's.

"What's up?" Dennis finally asks.

"You have to get rid of the new guy!" *Now I've done it. Opened my mouth. Now I'll have to tell them. And they'll think I'm crazy.*

"Rhonda told me about this afternoon, but we can't get rid of somebody just 'cause you don't like him." Dennis smiles and leans back against the counter.

That burns me. "It's not that. Just trust me and lose him!"

"Trust works both ways. You're going to have to trust me and tell me why," Dennis says with a straight face.

I take a big breath and let it out. "He wants to dip his pen in company ink." *There, I said it. It's done. Please let him believe me.*

"What? I don't understand what you mean."

"For Christ's sakes, Dennis, he made a pass at me!" I can taste angry bile in my throat.

Dennis looks stunned. "Are you okay?"

The word "okay" lights my fuse. "Okay? Sure, I'm fine. It's not me I'm worried about. Ask Victoria about her story. If he hits on her or Lily . . . I'll kill him."

"Okay, Marty . . ."

"But first I would shoot him in the –"

"Marty!"

"Kneecaps and then I would cut his –"

"OKAY."

"And feed them to starving dogs –"

"I get the POINT!"

"AND MAKE HIM WATCH!" I say, just in case he doesn't.

Dennis looks like he's in pain.

"Aren't you going to ask me how I really feel about this?"

"No."

Dennis believes me . . . believes me.

"D" Day

"He's here, Marty," Jackie says, as she glides across the room and settles on my bed like a big manta ray. Usually she bulldozes and bounces. She isn't my Jackie today; she is someone else's. She also isn't saying anything else.

"Okay, Jackie, I give up. Who's *he?*" I say, looking at the floor.

"Your father."

A pause. "Like I said, who's he?" My hands start to shake. I watch as the ray rests, quietly waiting for the wave to crash on its head. "I can't believe you didn't warn me!" A tremor creeps into my voice.

"I didn't know he was coming. He was in LA and decided to fly down."

"How convenient." I rip a hangnail off my thumb.

"It wasn't, actually. He canceled meetings to come here."

"Now you're defending him? But why not, huh, Jackie? He's the one paying you."

Jackie just looks at me, armor shining – the daggers bounce off her.

"Well, we better go see him, Jack. Time is money and I'll bet the meter is running."

On the way down in the elevator, I count while I breathe. In for ten. Out for ten. I fight the urge to gulp the stale recycled air. My hands and the shaking. *I hate the shaking.* We stop at the basement and the doors scrape their metal and open wide.

As we approach the office, Jackie just reaches out and opens the door. No key this time, just a side step like in a dance, a practiced look, and an open palm to make me go first.

I march two paces, front and center, to my father. I must look like a nutcracker – jaw clenched, arms at my side. My father rises, places a hand on the side of my arm, and mechanically kisses my hair. He misses my forehead because he is looking at Jackie. I move a quarter step right so he can take both of her hands in his. A warm shake and Jackie asks us to sit down. Then nothing.

The silence becomes heavy, sweating, and tight. I put my feet on my chair and my knees to my chest. My position doesn't prompt any comment, though I'm waiting for a "sit properly," or something. Question – *Why are we putting ourselves through this?* Answer – *Dad is here because he is paying for it. I'm here because Jackie said I had to be. And Jackie is here because it is her job. Her job is to deliver us.*

"Thank you for coming, Martin. I'm sure it took a lot of juggling to get here," Jackie says.

"It did and I'm leaving on the 4:30, back to New York," my father says in his so-make-it-fast voice.

Great, he just got here and he's already leaving. Fine, the sooner the better. They start talking about the weather and all I can hear is *blah, blah, blah.* The air vent has thirteen slats.

"Marty, are you with us?" Jackie asks, calling me back.

"What?"

"I need you to stay here in this room," Jackie says, leaning forward.

"Yeah," I lie. I wrap my arms around my knees.

"Say yes, Marty. And sit properly."

"Yes, Mar . . . yes, Dad. Sorry." My feet hit the floor. My hands fall in my lap.

"Marty, why do you think you're here?" Jackie pulls her starter trigger.

"I don't know." The three words Jackie hates. They tell her I'm not leaving the gate.

"Try," Jackie coaxes.

"Because I'm sick." *Let the games begin.*

"Yes, you were admitted because you're sick. You're here to get better. But I'm asking why you are here today, right now, in my office?"

"Did I have a choice?" I say, my eyes locked on hers.

"Okay. You win. Now try this one. Why do you think your father is here?"

"Good question." *Wish I knew the answer.*

"He had a choice, Marty."

"Therapists aren't supposed to make statements," I fire back.

"My office, my rules. I know you think he does things just because he's paying for them. But why does he keep paying?"

"You can't do this."

"Why does he pay, Marty?"

I move to sit on my hands. I stare at the floor. *No answer there. I've been played. I hate Jackie.* And I hate myself for losing control. The hating is an escape. Jackie lets me go.

"Okay, Martin, I'll ask you. Why do you pay?"

"Because I have to," Dad says, shifting in his chair.

The words come out of his mouth and stick in my throat. They choke me till I start crying.

"Why?" Jackie ignores me.

"The insurance has run out and nobody else can."

"Why not just leave? Walk away?"

What the hell? Well, there you go, Martin. There's your out.

"I guess it's my turn," he replies. He clears his throat and begins to search his jacket.

Yep, find your keys. Get in your car. Get on your plane. Have a nice life.

Jackie is cool, unaffected, professional. She waits till he finds what he is looking for. Not keys, but a crisp, white linen handkerchief. Never used. "Your turn for what?" she asks.

He finally answers, "My turn to break down."

"Is that what you think has happened to Marty – she's broken down?"

"I don't know . . . I've made some mistakes and I guess she has paid for them." He holds the cloth to his eyes like a blindfold.

I can't have heard him right. *Did he say he made a mistake? Did I pay for something?* My heart is racing. I've been somewhere like this before. A long time ago.

Daddies don't cry, I mouth silently, looking at my dad.

"I'm sorry, Marty, I can't hear you," Jackie says, as if nothing is wrong.

"Daddies don't cry," I say out loud. . . . The water brakes.

"Go on, Marty." Jackie waits. Dad looks up.

"The last time I saw my dad cry, he went away. I was three. He was leaving me. I didn't know that then. All I knew was that daddies didn't cry. I don't want him to leave. I . . . I need him."

"Tell him that," Jackie says, nodding towards Dad.

I can't speak. *How am I supposed to talk to this stranger who crumbled before my eyes?* I'm used to Martin the wall. The wall I bang my head against. The one that hits back with violent silence.

Breaking

I calculate what Dad's tears are costing. Multiply the number of tears per minute by the amount that you get when you divide sixty into one hundred and fifty. But the tears are coming too fast to count. I figure even Einstein couldn't calculate what those tears cost Dad.

Jackie wraps us up gently. She does all the talking about the time being up and that she hopes to see my dad again. I don't speak till we are all standing on the other side of the crying room door.

"I don't want you to leave, Dad," I say.

"I'm not leaving you," he replies.

"I mean today. I don't want you to leave today."

"I have to."

"Did you have to leave when I was little?" I'm feeling brave because Jackie is still with us, but she says nothing. The session is over.

Dad sighs. "That's a long story. I'll make you a deal. I'll change my flight to a later one and you will come out to lunch with me."

Morsel for morsel. What a dealmaker.

"No offense, Jackie, but I'd rather pay for lunch than for you," Dad says.

"None taken. I think it's a good idea." Jackie smiles.

"Hurry up and change, Marty. I'm starving." He pushes me down the hall.

I turn around and look at my dad. He is grinning.

"Ha-ha! Very funny." I turn again and leave them in the hallway. I push the elevator button – there is only one. Up. The doors open; I step inside.

I arrive at my floor and decide to spread my unexpected good cheer to the residents of the other units. I don't know why. I just know I'm alive; they should know I am alive too. Through the safety glass of the loony bin gates, I yell, "Just 'cause you're paranoid doesn't mean that somebody isn't after you."

A commotion starts with a lot of "I told you so's" and yelling of "Get away from me; I know who you really are – who you really work for!" Jesus is standing in the hall, looking to God for guidance. He falls to his knees and pees himself. I imagine God giving the command, "Thou shalt bend thy knee and wet thy pants!" That can't be all he said because Jesus looks heavenward again, nods his agreement, turns and narrows his eyes at me through the glass, and yells, "Sinner!" and then he cries for me. Maybe Jesus is the one with the most on the ball.

I walk down the hall to the druggie and dry-out unit. It isn't a locked unit, so I open the gates to their hell and yell in my best evangelistic voice, "Alcohol Devil be gone!"

Only one person yells anything and that is, "Fuck off!"

By the time I get to my unit doors, I have run out of things to say. As I pass the nurses' station, Dennis is filling in some report and holds up his pointer finger, indicating I should stop and wait till he finishes something. I keep walking and hold up my middle finger.

"You're a real little spark plug today, huh, Marty?" Dennis yells after me. News travels fast. Faster than I can walk.

"My dad cried." I throw him a bone.

"And that puts you in a good mood?"

"*Duh!*"

"Why?"

I stop at my door to think about that. And then tell Dennis the truth. "It means he's human, unlike you." I jump inside my room and slam the door shut to make sure I get the last word.

I change into a white summer dress; sit on the bed and wait.

I start thinking about what happened in Jackie's office and about going to lunch. Going to lunch with Dad. It's too much. My mind wanders to when I used to train horses.

When you are trying to gentle a horse, you perform the niceties: "How you doin', boy?" Pat, pat, rub the back, scratch the top of the head where the halter goes, talking the whole time. What you're really saying is, "Don't worry, boy, nothing is going to happen, nothing to be scared of, we're not going to do anything." Once he gets used to that, you say to him, "Well, since we're here and all friendly and everything, why don't we just go for a walk or something? Gee, the ring looks like a good place. Not enough room for me to run around, and I don't need the exercise, so I'll just stand in the middle and you can run around me, okay?" So the horse does this for a while and thinks this is not so bad. And then you say, with surprise in your voice, "Oh, boy, look at that. A saddle. A saddle just sitting on the fence, with nothing to do. Let's go look at that for a bit. Let's smell it, check it out. Not so bad. A little scary maybe 'cause it's something new, but new is good, right?" And the horse goes, *Okay, if you say so, I trust you. You haven't hurt me yet, so you must be on my side.* You go, "That's right and you know what? I think this saddle would look better on your back than on this fence, whatdaya say?" The horse looks at you like you're nuts, but if you're not afraid of it he thinks, *I'll go along, after all it is just going to sit on my back, right?* So you put it on him and he shakes a little bit. You rub him and talk to him and you are being so nice that he wants to impress you, so he stops making a fuss. That's when you grab the cinch and yank it up tight around his belly so he can't get the saddle off. If he starts to throw a fit, you hop the fence and let him fight it out, let him buck and kick and scream and roll on it and rub on the fence with this thing that was supposed to be okay, but then turned into something else. And when he's had it out with the clingy, smelly thing on his back, he stops and puts his head down. He's deciding whether to forgive you or not. And finally he comes over to the fence and you climb back into the ring and make up. He looks at you as if to say, *I can't believe you did that to me. I trusted you.* Then you rub his neck, and apologize and tell him how brave he was and how good he is, and you hold his head until he lets you kiss him on the muzzle without him trying to bite you first. You take off the saddle and put it on the fence. And the horse says, *Thank God that's over.* And you don't tell him that tomorrow you are going to do the same thing, only this time you're going to get on top of him and ride him through his tantrum till he gives up, till his spirit breaks if necessary. And after you break his spirit, you break the news. (And you don't let him see that it breaks your heart to do this because you have to at least appear to be the boss, so he'll do what you tell him and not question you.) You look him in the eye and say, "We're not friends. This is work. This is the way it has to be. I wish it could be different, but it can't. You've got your job and I've got mine. Let's get to work."

I want to run to Jackie. Tell her I understand. Tell her I'm sorry she is not my friend. I want to tell her I'm ready to work. Because I understand. And everybody has to figure that out when they're ready.

Lunch with Dad

"We'll have a table by the window, please," Dad says.

The hostess leads us past the stuffed sailfish on the walls. The restaurant isn't that busy. Too nice a day to be inside.

"Take your hat off," Dad says, as he sits.

"Can't . . . I'll have hat head." *Sorry, Dad. I'll need it when the crying starts. Don't let them see you cry. Wear a wide brim hat. Never cut your bangs. Only cry real hard in the shower . . . those are the rules.*

"Alright, what would you like?" Dad asks from behind his menu.

"I don't know." From anyone else, that would be a normal answer. From me, it's usually a stall tactic. But today, I really don't know. I want to order an entrée that says *I'm glad you're here, thanks for coming today, I'm ready to try harder.* "I'll have a salad." *Great. I just said go to hell.*

Dad's menu hits his bread plate and I drop my head. He can yell at the hat if he wants to. The waitress shows up. I can only see her up to the neck. Black shoes, black pants, white blouse, and a black bow tie. She looks like a referee for a boxing match. She doesn't know she just stepped into the ring. Her hair and her voice are blonde.

"My name is Sandy. What can I get for you?" asks Sandy, our golden retriever.

Silence. Dad, and his manners, and Sandy, and Etiquette Emily What's-her-name, and everybody in the whole restaurant wants me to order first. But I can't. Dad inhales his frustration and exhales his order.

"I'll have the steamed lobster with linguine and grilled vegetables . . . and *my daughter* will have a salad."

I look up and smile at Dad. He smiles back. Kind of.

"Your daughter, well, I thought there was a young lady under that hat! What kind of dressing would you like on your salad?"

"I'll have –"

"Dress it up with a rib eye steak, medium well, with cognac butter on top and a baked potato with butter and sour cream." I'm stunned. Sandy is confused. Dad clarifies. "You don't have to put all of that on the salad. Just put the food on a plate. The salad on the side. Oh, and blue cheese dressing on the salad."

Sandy looks relieved. "Your father is a funny guy." She laughs and scans his hand for a wedding ring. No gold. Not even a tan line. A pink frosted smile slides across her face. Sandy puts her hand on Dad's shoulder. "Can I show you our wine list?"

"Sure."

She snuggles up to him with the list. Like she's showing him the color of the curtains she picked out for their bedroom. Something in a nice Chardonnay.

I reach over and touch Dad's hand. He jerks it away like I burned him with a cigarette. It breaks up their party.

"And what would you like to drink, honey?" Sandy asks.

Now that I'm "the daughter," I'm "honey." And she's already dreaming about being my stepmother.

"I want a Diet Coke," I say, but she's back to staring at her new fiancé.

My father snaps her out of her fantasy. "Would you mind putting our order in? We're in a bit of a rush. Thanks."

The only bells you're going to hear today are the cook's . . . honey.

"You can have the Diet Coke, but I want the steak and potato eaten . . . all of them."

"Yes, sir." *I'm sure I'll enjoy it, sir. Please can I have some more, sir?*

"Don't 'yes, sir' me like I'm making you eat dog dirt. Your mother said this is the best restaurant in Seaport Village. She said you like it here."

"You talked to Mom?"

"From Jackie's office, while you were getting changed."

"Oh."

"I'm sorry about what happened back –"

"S'okay, Dad. We call her office the crying room. I'm sure she has a tear-quota in her contract. But she'll probably get a bonus for you."

"That's not what I'm talking about. I'm sorry that you remember me leaving. About what happened back when you were little."

I hold my breath, then let out the question that never has an answer: "What happened?"

Dad turns away to look out the window. Studies the boats in the marina. "I don't know. But we loved each other. Once."

Duh! Big revelation. "I figured that Dad. Why else would you get married?"

"Because of you."

"What do you mean?" I ask, and look right at him while he fishes the bay for an answer.

"We were married in August. You were born that December. You do the math."

I count on my fingers under the table. *August, September, October, November, December.* "Was I premature?"

"No. You were a week late."

"Oh." *Oh, my God. That's a nice little seventeen-year secret.*

"Your mother was four months pregnant when we got married. We were from a small town. It was rough on her. She didn't have a lot of support. Even from her own family. She was supposed to go to teachers college and I was already in art school. But all that changed."

"And I've been paying for it ever since," I mumble.

Dad turns back to the table. "What was that?" he asks.

"I said, it makes a lot of sense."

"What does?"

"Well, a couple of years ago I asked Mom about sex. I thought we'd have a little mother-daughter chat. She went ballistic. She said if I had sex, or if she found out I had had sex, before I was eighteen, she'd throw me out of the house. I never understood why she got so mad. She knew I was taking sex-ed at school; she signed the form . . . now it all makes sense."

"She was just trying to protect you."

"I'm not the one who needed protection."

"Very funny."

Sandy shows up with the drinks. "Did I miss the joke?" she asks.

"Yeah, I just found out when the rabbit died," I answer.

"Oh, I thought I heard 'funny,' not 'bunny.' I'm sorry your rabbit died. I'll be right back with your lunch."

Dad chokes on his wine and Sandy scampers away.

The food is coming. Dad's lightened up. Roll with it. "So really, if it weren't for me, you'd be a starving artist instead of a venture capitalist."

"Not likely, but speaking of starving . . ."

Sandy is here with our lunch. "I asked the chef to pick out the biggest steak for you. You could use a little meat on your bones," she says, and places a side of beef in front of me and a candy-apple crustacean in front of my father.

The lobster face is staring at me across the table. Its eyes are bulging out at the size of my steak.

"Can I do anything else for you?" Sandy asks me.

"No, you've done quite enough. THANK YOU."

"More wine?"

"I'm fine, thanks."

"Well, enjoy your lunch then."

"Oh, we will," Dad says, and narrows his eyes at me.

Baked potato – two hundred twenty calories. Sour cream, two tablespoons – fifty-two calories. Butter, four pats – one hundred and sixty. One huge steak – at least a thousand calories. Diet Coke – one calorie.

I take a big drink.

"Dig in, Marty."

"Dad, I . . ."

My father breaks his lobster in half. It looks like I'm going to be next if I don't start eating. We're getting along. I don't want him to leave. I slice off a piece of steak, shove it in my mouth and bite down. Juice and butter squish out between my lips, run down my chin, and drip onto the front of my dress. My white dress. I swallow. *What a pig I am.*

"I'm proud of you, Marty."

"For eating a piece of meat?"

"For lots of things."

"Name one."

78

"Okay, let's see – Junior National Honor Society, being first chair flutist for the one year you played in the band, first girl to play football on the boys team, winning the city's storefront window-painting contest last Christmas, and all the horses you got on that everyone said couldn't be ridden. You got on and stayed on. You always pick the mission impossible. You haven't let anything or anyone stop you from attaining your goals. The list is impressive. It's also very scary. Your success terrifies me. Because if you choose to continue *this*, I've no doubt you will succeed. But you can't win by not eating. It makes it hard to love you, Marty." Dad stops and realizes he hasn't touched his food.

Sure, build me up just to tear me down. I hate this food and I hate you. That's it. Get mad. Get mad and you won't cry. "So you'll only love a winner." *That should do it. He'll storm out now and we'll see who wins.*

Dad wipes the foam from his mouth and throws down his napkin. "You want me to love you unconditionally! But what about the conditions you place on me – fly down here, Dad; meet with a therapist, Dad; do this and I'll eat, Dad!"

"I never asked you . . ." I can't talk. The tears are coming.

"Didn't you, Marty? Ten pounds in six weeks! Big deal! I think a lot of pampering goes on in that hospital and for the same amount of money I could send you to a spa, and you could eat at the best restaurants in town, taken there by your own God damn limousine!"

"I'm sorry about the money."

79

"It's not about money; I can always make money, but I can't make you. And I can't love you like this. Once survival is assured, I can afford to invest."

So now I'm a stock option that has to prove itself before he'll buy in.

Sandy rushes up to the table. "I forgot your salad."

"It's okay. She's had enough."

Dad finishes his wine. "Go wash your face and I'll pay the bill."

I can't get to the bathroom fast enough. I shove through the door. Nobody home. I go into the last stall. Lock the door, grab a wad of toilet paper, shove my face into it and cry and choke on the lint, and pray that no one comes in – as quietly as I can.

Someday

We walk out of the restaurant. Dad turns and heads towards the docks. I follow a little behind and keep my head down. He sits on a bench facing the bay and pats the paint-chipped wood beside him. I sit and look up. A wave of birds washes over the sky and breaks the silence.

"You see that big sloop out there, moored all by itself?" Dad asks.

"Yes."

"It's called a Procrastination 54."

"Looks like a slice of the moon fell into the water and someone stuck a big fork in it."

"I don't know about the moon, but it is a piece of heaven. There are only five of them in the world. The guy who builds them takes forever. He'll have to live to three hundred and ten to fill his orders. And he doesn't even let you name them. You sign a contract saying you'll never change what he christens them." Dad points to the sloop. "That one's name is *Someday*."

"How do you know all of this?"

"I chartered one once in the Virgin Islands. Schools of dolphins, blue-green lagoons, and turtles that fly under-water. You'd love it. The boat's name was *Tomorrow*."

"I'd like to see it . . ."

"I'd love to show it to you."

I take off my hat.

Dad takes my hand in both of his and puts them on his knee. And we stare across the water at *Someday*.

DAY 54
AUGUST 6

Starfish

Every day is the same in here. No seasons. No sense of time. It's like I'm living on the Starship Enterprise. Only my schedule is different.

Get up.

Weigh in.

Pig out.

Mess with my mind.

Have a snack of cottage cheese.

Let someone else mess with my mind.

Eat lunch.

Take a shower and try to scrub off the oil from the lasagna that is leaking out of my skin.

Draw some pictures of what's going on "inside."

Have a snack of Oreo cookies and half-pint of milk.

Think of someone I can call who is still talking to me – which is no one.

Waddle into dinner.

Roll back to my room. Try to have a nice visit with whoever shows up, even if it's always Mom.

Sneak in a few push-ups, sit-ups.

Have a last snack of peanut butter and crackers and milk.

Watch some TV.

Have nothing to say when the night nurse asks me if I want to talk about today.

Do deep-knee bends while brushing my teeth.

Look in the full-length mirror on the back of the bathroom door.

Hate myself.

Go to sleep.

Every day the same. Except when I step outside. As soon as I leave the capsule, there is a day waiting for me. With a name. Like Monday. And certain things you have to do. Like buy a bathing suit and go to lunch at a restaurant afterward. On Monday, Nurse Jane took only Bonnie, Katherine, Lily, and me bathing suit shopping. Because the other girls have been to camp before and completed their badges in shopping and lunching. We were supposed to be supportive and encouraging. Depend on each other, like the sailors would when they had to keelhaul a shipmate. The one being punished had a rope tied around him and was then thrown overboard, dragged under the boat and up the other side as fast as his mates could pull. Monday we were tortured without getting wet.

Wednesday is for getting wet. Today is Wednesday. We have waited our one hour after lunch, been shipped through the pouring rain in our yellow submarine to the pool, and now are going swimming.

Catwoman has been left behind – fear of the water. Rhonda chases Rose, Bonnie, Elizabeth, Victoria, Jamie, Katherine, Nancy, Lily, and me into the change room. We scatter into any hiding place we can find – bathroom stalls and private showers. Victoria and Nancy fight over the handicap change room with a lock. All our suits are black one-pieces, except Lily's, which is blue. The boutique didn't have any pink one-pieces you could rinse in a shot glass. Only bikinis. And we didn't leave any fingerprints on them.

Rhonda claps to get our attention. The echo off all the green tiles startles us. "Sorry 'bout that. You have to take a shower before you swim. Do it in the communal area. Nobody is going to come in here or the pool. We have only forty-five minutes because you guys took so long getting ready, so make the showers short." Rhonda looks around. "Where's Lily?"

I know where she is – stalling behind the curtain of a cubby. "I'll get her," I say.

"No." Rhonda looks afraid to lose a fish from the school.

"Maybe she needs help."

"Okay, but no fooling around." Rhonda nods.

I do a silly walk to where Lily is holed up. I can't knock on a curtain, so I shuffle my flip-flops to let her know I'm coming. "Hey, Lil, what's up?"

"Nothing." Her voice isn't big enough to bounce off the walls.

"It's kind of cold in here, maybe in the pool too. I brought an extra T-shirt if you want to wear it."

"Okay."

I run to my bag, grab the T-shirt, and throw it over the curtain rod.

Lily comes out wearing my shirt down to her knees and a towel over her head. "Thanks," she says, her voice muffled by the thick towel.

"Come on, let's go swimming. You can show me your dog paddle." I pull her into the shower for people with wheelchairs and hose both of us down. Rhonda too. By accident. I didn't know she was waiting for us.

She looks at her pants. "Get in that pool," she says slowly.

I push through the door that says THIS WAY TO POOL and tow Lily behind me, down a tiled corridor. The chlorine smells a lot better than hospital bleach. Not as good as salt water, but it'll do. The humidity is an oasis away from the cold dry air of the institute. It figures that an indoor pool has been rented for us. Less chance of someone going AWOL. I don't think there are any walled beaches in San Diego.

It's a short walk to the poolside. I round the corner and stop dead. Lily bumps into me. I pull her around so she can see. The tropical storm has passed and through floor-to-ceiling windows and massive skylights, the sun pours in. The light bounces off the water and plays on the walls. In one corner by the deep end, clouds of steam float like gossamer scarves in the air above a Jacuzzi. Everyone except Jamie is in it, trying to burn off calories. Jamie is perched on the edge of the high diving board, her wings stretched out wide. She bends her knees and drives the board towards the water. She swings her arms in big circles. One more bounce and she is flying in the air. Up . . . up . . . a swan that is going to escape through the glass in the roof. Gravity finally gets a grip on her and she disappears into the water like a knife.

I'm dying to get into the water. But Lily won't budge.

Rhonda comes up beside me. "Go on. I'll look after this little guppy," she says, and leads Lily away.

I run on my toes, drop my towel at the last second, and do a shallow dive into the shallow end. I swim the breast-stroke underwater, all the way to the deep end. I break the surface to get the air I've run out of. Turning to look at the lifeguard sitting in her high chair beside the pool, I see she is smiling. Not yelling at me for breaking the two most basic rules of any pool: NO RUNNING, NO DIVING IN THE SHALLOW END.

I swim along the bottom with my eyes open. There is a ton of chemicals in the water. When I used to surf, I'd check out the reef below me in between waves. It doesn't hurt. It's an ocean of tears.

I surface at the side of the pool. "The chlorine is eating my eyeballs. Do you have a pair of goggles I can borrow?" I call up to the lifeguard.

"Sure." She unwraps a florescent orange pair from around the arm of her chair and tosses them down. "Have fun."

"Thanks." I snap them on and pull away in freestyle. One-two-three-four, roll my head to the side and force air and spray through my blowhole, grab some as I roll my face back into the water. Repeat. Over and over. I relax and pick up speed. Dive-flip-turn-slam my feet against the side and explode off the wall. Whip my body through the water with six dolphin kicks. As I come up for air, I can hear my coach's whistle blowing. The past rushing by me like the water. It gets louder.

I stop in the shallow end to shake the auditory hallucination from my head. Lily pokes me and points to Rhonda, who has a whistle in her mouth. The poor lifeguard is still attached to it by a cord around her neck. She is almost being pulled out of her chair by Rhonda, who has stopped blowing but is now beckoning me to come.

Rhonda looks red from her workout. "Pull back on the throttle, Marty. Take it down to cruising speed. No wake. Got it?"

"Yes, coach." I slide underwater and release the air from my lungs to watch the bubbles go up as I sink. Four walls close back in on me.

Sitting on the bottom, I watch Jamie dive again. She is just as graceful from down under. Motion out the side of my goggles turns my eyes. I see Lily's legs moving furiously like little eggbeaters, whipping her white T-shirt into a meringue. I swim slowly underwater and grab her ankles. I hear a muted squeal. I rise out of the water like the creature from the black lagoon. Lily's clutching onto her small yellow inner tube and giggling at full volume.

"You scared me!" Lily says, eyes sparkling.

"You liked it."

Lily smiles full of electricity.

"Ditch the tube, Lil, and come swimming with me."

Her smile goes dead.

"What's wrong?"

"I can't swim."

"You grew up on a beach in La Jolla and you never . . ." I don't finish because Lily is turning away. I put my hand on her tube and hold her in place. "Can you float without the ring?"

No answer.

Cupping my hands, I pour water over her head so we can both pretend she isn't crying. I have to ask her a question, but my plan won't work unless I get the right answer. I put my forehead to hers. "Do you trust me?"

Lily nods up and down, rubbing our noses together.

As I pull her to the steps, the other girls file past to the change room. I look at the clock – 2:50 P.M. Rhonda comes to the side and squats down. "You guys want to stay?" she asks.

"Yes," Lily says.

"Okay, but no torpedoing around the pool, Marty."

"I won't sink anything."

"I'll see you both in ten minutes," Rhonda says, and leaves us alone.

I stand Lily on the bottom step and remove her lifesaver. The water comes up to her chest and so does the T-shirt. "We have to take this off too."

She lets me. Maybe it's just her suit, but her skin looks a little blue.

"Are you cold? Do want to go in the Jacuzzi?"

"No. Let's go swimming." She looks scared but excited.

I put her arms around my neck and she jumps on my back. Clings to me like a koala. We move away from the steps, but stay close enough in case she panics.

"Let's start by floating. The easiest way is on your stomach. Take a big breath, puff out your cheeks like this." I demonstrate. "Let your arms and legs hang loose and just lie in the water. It's called dead man's float."

"I don't like the sound of that," Lily says, and hugs me tighter.

"Okay, okay, Lily, you're choking me."

"Sorry," Lily says, into my neck.

I lower us both into the water. "Relax. I'm not going to let anything happen to you. I'm going to hold you up so you can float on your back. I won't let go of you, but you have to let go of me. Alright?"

Lily doesn't answer. She lets her arms slide from around my neck and stops squeezing with her legs. I put my hands on her ribs to turn her on her back. Her face looks as rigid as her little body.

"Take some slow deep breaths. I'm going to put one hand under your neck to support your head and one hand just above your bum. You're doin' great, Lil. Breathe. Now push your tummy up towards the ceiling. That's it. Keep breathing. Stick your arms and legs out to the side. Point your toes and fingers. Great. You got it. You're doin' the starfish!"

A smile crawls across Lily's face.

I'm only holding her up with one finger. "You're practically solo. Okay if I join you?"

Lily nods *yes*.

I float on my back beside her. The water around me turns to body temperature. I can't tell where I end and the pool begins. I think about Lily. About the brittle stars I used to see in the tide pools. Little starfish with round bodies and spindly legs. They don't do well in captivity. If the conditions aren't right, they just dissolve.

I take my hand from underneath Lily and put my fingers through hers.

DAY 57
AUGUST 9

Journal Entry # 2

I'm thinking that Katz is not so stupid. I know he's not stupid. Just stupid about me. Not stupid. Ignorant. Lacking knowledge. So you want to know? Here is a little tidbit for the cat.

They let me out for good behavior. So I did something bad. Tonight I went to a party with Katherine. I didn't know anybody else and I didn't care. I got out – that was the point. Out. I had a glass of wine on the outside. Got drunk on the inside. All those alcohol molecules petting the empty shells of my brain cells. *After* they've obliterated what's inside. Stroking them and saying I'm sorry . . . I'm sorry. Innocent, fragile little brain cells. Oh, well. So long, boys. Go down with your ships and take your memories with you. Every time I have a drink, I think about my mother . . . wonder if I'm like her . . . afraid that I am her.

One glass of wine. If Katz reads this, he'll be shopping for tequila. A little *to-kill-ya* for my journal and me.

. . . here, kitty kitty.

Signed, M.

Breaking Glass

Lily goes first. Gained a quarter pound from yesterday, she skips off to her room to change.

"Step up, Marty," Dennis says with something that sounds like "I'm sorry."

Sometimes I think Dennis hates the morning weigh-ins as much as we do. Like the hangman who hates his job.

I look behind me. There they are – the prisoners all lined up, waiting for their turn at the scaffold. Some are praying. They can already feel the weight of *the number* hanging around their necks. Choking them till they can't breathe. It's only a number. A number on a scale that doesn't mean anything. *No matter what it says, I'm not going to care. I'm tired of caring about a stupid number.* Still, I look back again to see who will see my face when I meet my maker.

"Do you want to go to the other room to weigh in?" Dennis says, trying to be sensitive. It pisses me off.

"No." I stand up straight. Cheek bones up. Rib cage out. Shoulder blades back. And I take two steps forward till my bare feet stay still on the steel long enough for Dennis to weigh me. *100 pounds.* I take one step back. *100 pounds.*

"Are you okay?" Dennis knows the answer, but asks anyway.

I can barely hear him. *100 pounds.* The number I've worked so hard to avoid. *I don't care. I don't care.* The boulder of 100 pounds I used all my strength to squeeze under and stay there. *What's the big deal with 100? I don't care.* Now I am three digits instead of two. Two is always under 100. I've lost control of my two-digit world. 100 might as well be 300. There is no difference.

"I need to take your blood pressure and some blood," another nurse says.

"Later." I start for my room.

"We need to –" she tries again.

"Later!" Dennis barks.

My legs are marching to the cadence of *I don't care.* My eyes are busy. Searching, scanning like one of those red lasers on the scope of a sniper's rifle. *Where is the glass?* I pace the whole unit. The only glass in here has little veins of metal running through it.

"You can't get there from here. We're not like the other glass. Hit us as hard as you like. We'll just smash into a thousand pieces. Blunt pieces. Useless. They'll just call the janitor. There will be no bloodletting by us. No visible scars. Maybe some crushed bones, but those will heal and still no one will see."

I'm so transparent even the windows can see through me. *This is nuts. Having a conversation with safety glass. This place is making me crazy.*

I walk quickly, quietly to my bathroom. Lock the door. Look hard into the eyes of the fat girl in the mirror.

Find a way back under a hundred pounds, Marty. Before you explode.

Cut my hair! No scissors. *Push-ups!* I get down into position. The cold of the floor shoots through my hands and up my arms like an electric shock. Energizes me. One hundred push-ups. *No slacking off. No matter what. GO!*

One . . . two . . . three . . . four . . . five . . .

A voice. "Marty? Are you in there? It's Dennis."

Eight . . . nine . . . ten . . .

"I know you're in there, Marty. I can hear you breathing. You have to stop. Not breathing, I mean. I mean, don't stop breathing, just stop whatever you're doing in there and come out and talk to me."

Sixteen . . . seventeen . . .

"If you don't come out, I'm going to have to come in. So come out and make life easier for both of us."

Life's . . . not . . . about . . . easy . . .

"Cripes!" Dennis says and leaves.

Twenty-five . . . twenty-six . . . twenty-seven . . . twenty-eight . . . twenty-nine . . .

Dennis is back. He jams a key into the lock and yells, "Last chance, Miss Black!"

Black . . . and . . . white . . . prepare . . . to . . . fight . . .

My arms give out and my face smacks the floor. The door flies open. Dennis falls to his knees and tries to get me into some Greco-Roman wrestling hold.

Forget this! I can't breathe. I push myself up and throw my head back.

Crack! Thunk!

"Shit!" Dennis says, and slowly lets go of me.

I scramble out from under him and get my back to the wall. Dennis falls back on his butt. He grabs the toilet with one hand and the back of his head with the other. Looks through squinty eyes at the sink that dented his head. Blood runs from his nose.

"I'm sorry, Dennis. I didn't mean to. . . . Do you think you broke it?"

"The sink? Who cares about the sink?" Dennis says and shuts his eyes.

"Not the sink! Your nose!"

"Oh. I don't know. I don't think *you* broke my nose." Dennis sounds like he has a cold, "But I'd like to know what you did to yours?"

I touch my nose, pull my hand away, and there is blood on it. Must be from the ceramic facial I gave myself before Dennis so rudely interrupted me in the spa.

"What the hell were you doing in here?" Dennis says.

"Nothing." *Just a little exercise.*

"So I've got a lot of pain for nothing?"

"I said I'm sorry. You surprised me."

"Maybe you're right. I should have known better than to tackle a skinny little salamander like you."

Dennis raises his eyebrows and turns his head toward the door. Footsteps. "Incoming," he whispers and smiles.

Nurse Jane pops her face around the door. "GOOD MORNING, VIETNAM!"

"Morning, Janey," Dennis chirps.

"Dennis! What happened?"

"Just a little A.M. alligator wrestling to start off the day." Dennis laughs and chokes, which makes blood bubbles come out his nose.

Nurse Jane stares at him. Then at me. Then at him again. "Ugh," she says, and leaves.

"Good-bye, Janey!" I say, and laugh and blow some bubbles of my own. That starts the whole contest between me and Dennis to see who can gurgle and cough and say "ow" and swear and make little red balloons come out our noses.

Jane comes back with two Ziploc baggies full of ice. Tosses one to me and fires the other bag into Dennis's lap. He catches it within an inch of the life of his boys. Dennis stops laughing.

Jane smirks and says, "Now that I have your attention, do you want me to finish the weigh-in? The girls are waiting."

"*Argh.* . . . Yeah. Would you mind? Thanks, Jane. I had forgotten about that." Dennis stretches his legs out across the bathroom floor.

I had forgotten about it too. *Thanks for nothing, Jane.*

Jane leaves to go weigh the chickens.

"Why the dark face, Marty?" Dennis asks.

"Nothing."

"Would that be a hundred pound nothing?"

That's me. A hundred pound nothing.

"Come on. You broke my nose. You owe me a break-through."

"Stop trying to push my buttons. You wouldn't understand."

"Yes, I would . . . ah, shit. . . . You're right, Marty. I wouldn't. And I never will. You want the truth?"

No, lie to me. Like everyone else.

"Here's the truth. I think this not eating, or eating and puking, is nuts. I tried starving myself, you know. I lasted a whole day. And it was hell. I tried throwing up too. I wanted to try and understand something. But I don't. I think it's crazy. Doing drugs makes more sense."

"I don't do drugs."

"Of course you don't. You wouldn't do them because you don't control drugs. They control you."

"Maybe."

"Maybe at weigh-in this morning, the scale took away your ninety-nine pound drug and gave you a one hundred pound shot of reality. And you flipped. So, drugs, numbers, scales – what's the difference? It's just the poison you pick."

"You going somewhere with this, Dennis?" I shift because my bum is falling asleep.

"The question is, are *you*?"

"I don't have a lot of options," I say to the floor.

"Sure you do. A) You could leave here today. B) Lose the weight you've gained, or C) Just kill yourself and get it over with."

"Those choices weren't on my admit sheet when my mom brought me in."

"They weren't in writing, but they're in your head." Dennis rubs his.

"What if I tell Nurse Brown you told me I could go kill myself?" I say, staring him in the face.

"I'd claim temporary insanity. Or just deny it." He looks for a dry patch on the washcloth he's holding.

"You'd lie?"

"You can be a royal pain in the ass. But for you, anything. I'll even help you get out of here."

"And go where?"

"Anywhere. What does it matter?" Dennis says and stands up. He leans over and puts out a hand to help me. "I'll get the forms signed and you can leave."

I'm shaking so much I can't move. My eyes are stinging. I feel sick to my stomach.

"Come on, Marty. It's over." He grabs my arm and jerks me up to my feet.

The sudden motion forces me to throw up the truth: "I'm afraid of what I might do on the outside."

Dennis pulls me into a desperate hug. "So someone else cares about you besides me."

"Nothing personal, Dennis, but I hate you."

"That's the nicest thing you've ever said to me." He squeezes me tighter.

DAY 74
AUGUST 26

Hiroshima

"What time is it?" I ask the room. No answer. *Must be late.* I'm always the last one up. The morning "concierge" always complains about having to come and wake me personally.

They used to yell, from their desk, through the little box behind my bed. Until I mashed wet toilet paper into the tiny holes of the speaker. It made their voices sound like Charlie Brown's teachers. It was funny till they found out. They told me I had to clean it. I said it would take forever. They said that was my problem. Three weeks ago, I solved my problem permanently.

I asked for a toothbrush to clean the holes, and to scrape off the paper-mâché, a knife from the kitchen. They gave me the dullest one they could find. I used the knife to unscrew the faceplate and put it under running water. My art project washed away in a couple of seconds. I used the plastic toothbrush to pull out and jam up as many wires as I could. Got another wad of toilet paper and stuffed it inside the box. Screwed the faceplate back on with the knife. The whole job took five minutes tops. Thought I must be going soft because the first time I'd messed with the speaker I'd broken one of the rules – ALWAYS DO YOUR DAMAGE AND HIDING ON THE INSIDE, SO ON THE OUTSIDE EVERYTHING LOOKS PERFECT. For the next twenty-five minutes, I did sit-ups in the bathroom to the chant of "screw you."

Well, I don't feel like sit-ups today. I feel like crap. All achy and clammy and big. My nightgown is sticking to my back with sweat and my mouth feels like someone filled it with glue. I give my teeth a good tongue-lashing, but it doesn't help much. I open one eye to check the clock over the door. It slowly comes into focus. Ten after six o'clock. A.M. I roll my head and scan the room to see if any inmates escaped in the night. *Nope. All here and accounted for.* Catwoman curled in a little ball at the foot of her bed. Katherine sleeping like a drooling angel, her praying hands trapped between her head and her pillow.

I've got to get up. Go to the bathroom. Then go back to bed and stay there for the rest of the day. I'll miss group therapy. *What a shame.*

I throw the covers off and jump out of bed. Five quick steps to the bathroom. I wheel around and close the door behind me. Turn around and grab the cold sides of the sink. *Dizzy. Moved too fast.* I bend over and hug the sink and put my forehead on the porcelain edge and suck air through my mouth. Feel better . . . as in "better get a bucket." *Open your eyes, stupid, and find something to focus on.* I open my eyes and look down at my feet on the tiles. The white tiles with blood on them. *What the hell? Are my gums bleeding again, my nose?* I look in the mirror to find the culprit. I snarl at myself but my fangs are white and my nose is cold and dry. I catch a glimpse of something red when I look into the mirror on the wall, past my face and into the reflection of the mirror on the door behind me. My nightgown is soaked in blood. Almost a perfect red bull's-eye is covering my butt.

"This can't be happening," I whisper. "No, no, no, no, No, NO!" I yell.

Two bed creaks. One small. One big.

"Shhhiiiit!" *Catwoman and Katherine.*

"Marty? Are you alright?" Katherine calls, with more fear than concern.

"Shit, Shit, SHIT!"

"Marty, what's wrong? Should I call a nurse?"

"NO! I'll be out in a minute," I shout through the door. I pull off my nightgown and shove it down into the garbage. Drop lots of clean toilet paper on top. Wipe the blood off the floor and my legs and some on my shoulder with more toilet paper and flush it down. My underwear. *What a mess.* I wad up the last of the roll and stuff into the crotch of my panties. Feels like I've got a tennis ball between my legs. Maybe they'll believe I swore because I ran out of paper . . . that I was just about to take a shower . . . any missed blood could be from shaving with my black market razor. *That's it.* Shower and shave . . . all evidence covered.

I walk out like a geisha, towel wrapped around me and tucked under my arms. "Katherine, I just –" I stop because Katherine isn't looking at me; she's staring at the floor. But Catwoman is sitting back on her haunches, eyes locked on my bed like she's seen a mouse. I look over too. Yes. I'd covered all the evidence. All the evidence except the Japanese flag I left exposed on my bed when I threw off the covers.

Now That We've Covered Toilet Paper, Here's 101 Uses for Tampons

"Marty –"

"Shut up, Katherine. Don't say anything." *Think, Marty. What are you going to do now?* I look over at

Catwoman. She's all balled up and facing the wall. *Katherine weighs enough; she's got to have something.* I turn to her. "Do you have any tampons?"

No answer. She just looks past me out the window.

"Katherine? . . . KATHERINE!"

"You told me not to say anything," Katherine says.

Fix it, Marty, fix it to get what you need so only three people will have to know. "Argh. Okay. I'm sorry, really very sorry. Can I please have some tampons?"

"No."

Fine, punish me, but I'm not going to suck up anymore. "Thanks for your help!"

"I don't have any. They took them away when I was admitted. You'll have to go to the nurse for some."

"I'd rather phone my father and ask him to fedex a box from New York."

"That'd be stupid," Katherine half laughs.

"Stupid, but easier, with less questions."

"That's true. What about your mom?"

I look at the clock. 6:30. *She won't be up yet. She can bring some before going to work.* I pull my blankets up to the head of the bed. Grab a T-shirt, sweatpants, and a clean pair of underwear. Quickly change in the bathroom and file the dirty panties under the pile of toilet paper.

"Katherine, it's not a big deal or anything, but –"

"I KNOW. Don't say anything. I know you call me chatty Kathy. . . . Don't worry, your little secret is safe with me," Katherine says, looking hurt. Again.

Yeah, right. "I'll be right back." I go into the hall and stand on my tiptoes to see down the corridor to the nurse's desk. *Nobody home.* I creep towards the lounge with the patients' phone. I crouch down in front of the desk and locate the nurse by sound. Weird lyrics to the tune of the Macarena come from the meds room.

> *Tryptophan, Lorazepam, Valium, and Ritalin*
> *Noooow you'll be sedated.*

She doesn't hear me go into the lounge and close the door. Too busy working on her second career. I pick up the phone, but can't remember the number. The phone is a spin dialer. Thousands of dollars a day for an old phone. I close my eyes and press my fingers on an imaginary keypad. *Got it.* Seven spins of the wheel of fortune.

"Hello?" Mom's froggy voice answers.

"Mom, I need –"

"Marty, what time is it? 6:40. What's wrong?"

"Nothing. Can you bring me a box of tampons before you go to work?"

"Did you get your period?"

Don't be smart. Be nice. "Yes."

"Well . . . congratulations. Do you know what to do?"

"YES! Can you just –"

"I don't think you're supposed to use tampons your first time."

"It's not my first time."

"When did you get it?"

"About three years ago. I just haven't had it in a while." *Two years and seven months to be exact.*

"Then this is good news, isn't it? I should call your father."

"NO! Mom, please, the things!"

"I'm showing a house at seven-thirty this morning. Just go to the nurse. I'm glad you called though; I've got to get up and put on the power suit. I'm sorry, honey."

"Forget it, Mom. Glad I could be of help," I say, and slam the phone down. The one good thing about old phones is that they're slammable.

You've run out of options, Marty. You have to go ask THEM.

The nurse is humming a new song when I come up to the desk. Takes her a minute to realize I'm there. "Where did you come from?" she asks as she checks behind me to see if anyone else magically appeared.

I take a deep breath. "I need a box of tampons."

"What for?"

"Arts and crafts."

She gives me the look.

"Okay. I'm constipated and need more fiber in my diet."

"What do you really need them for?" Another question, another look.

"Alright. I'm going to sew little lead balls into them and put them in every orifice so I can make my weight and get out of here."

"Did you get your period?"

"BINGO! We have a winner. Can I have the box now . . . please?"

"Just a minute." She goes to the meds room. Comes back and places two tampons on the counter in front of me.

"Only two? . . . I need a box."

"You can come back and get more."

"What if someone is around? Then they'll know. Then everyone will know!"

"What's wrong with everyone knowing?"

"You're right." I grab the microphone they use for announcements and flip the switch to ON. **"Attention, Kmart shoppers! Marty got her period. Cleanup on aisle five!"** I turn the mike off and glare at the nurse. "You happy? Now everyone knows how fat I am."

"You're not fat, Marty. Your *body fat* has just come up high enough for you to start menstruating again. This is a big day in your recovery. It'd be a good idea if you got used to it."

"You're not supposed to give advice – just ask questions!"

I arm myself with the two missiles and march down the hall. When I get to the room, Katherine is standing by my bed.

"I . . . ," Katherine starts.

"Not a word, Katherine, or I'll insert one of these down your throat and you'll suffocate and I won't change my mind and yank it out by the string!" I lock myself in the bathroom and sit down on the toilet. A nanosecond of free fall and I'm in the bowl along with one of the tampons. Someone had left the seat up. Because someone had cleaned it. And someone had also left a new roll of toilet paper and a washcloth on the sink. I fix myself up and come out.

"I made your bed and Catwoman did the litter box," Katherine says, and pulls back my covers. "Don't say anything. Just get in."

I crawl under the sheets and face the wall. She starts rubbing my back, and my eyes start leaking along with everything else.

"I'm sorry . . . ," I whisper into the mattress.

"I know you are. And I know you don't cry. You're just hormonal."

DAY 80
SEPTEMBER 1

Another postcard from Cherri.

> Hey, I'm not going to Princeton. I'm staying closer to home. By the time you get this I'll have started at University of San Diego. Maybe you can join me later. Here's my address and phone number. Call me. Love, Cherri

I put the card in my drawer.

Fun and Games

"What do you think all that sawing and hammering is?" Lily asks from across the table and pokes at her oatmeal.

"They're building coffins for us. So we can lie down in them and see what it feels like to be dead. It's a new form of therapy," I answer.

"I'm not getting in one. Everybody in my family is cremated," Bonnie says.

"Don't you mean everybody in your family is a cretin?" I ask.

"Very funny. I meant when someone in my family dies, they burn them."

"No problem. You get in your coffin. I'll get some of that lighter fluid they say is soup and pour it all over you. One match and up you'll go." I wink at Bonnie Bonfire. Smoke comes out her ears.

"I'm not getting in one either," Lily says, and looks like she's going to cry.

"I'm kidding, Lily," I say.

"I'm not going to die," Lily announces, but she doesn't look too sure.

"No, you're not, Lil. I won't let you."

"So I'm not going to practice," Lily says harshly to her shoes.

"It's just a joke." I laugh, but Lily's face doesn't look right.

"There is nothing funny about HELL!" Lily the evangelist shouts.

"Who . . . who said anything about hell?" I ask.

"My mother says lots about it. If she was here, she'd tell you too."

"If she was here, I'd tell her where to go."

"You'd burn for that," Lily says.

Actually I think I'd get brownie points from God if I told Lily's mother off. I'm going to burn for a million other things though.

Lily looks pink underneath her sweaty bangs.

"Forget about it . . . let's talk about something else."

The devil leaves Lily and she slumps in her chair.

I walk to the window and rest my elbows on the sill and put my head in my hands and cover my eyes like I'm counting to ten for a game of tag.

"The noise in here is enough to drive you crazy," Katherine says.

I whisper to the window, "Well, we won't have to worry about anybody getting carsick . . . 'cause it'll be a real short trip."

Birkenstock clogs clomp into the dining room. I keep facing the window. I already know who it is.

"Please sit down." Brown's voice is cool.

I turn and slide to the floor.

"In a chair."

"What? In a chair?" I repeat.

"Sit down in a chair."

"You know, you just sit in a chair. You don't have to say sit 'down.' The down is redundant." I stay where I am.

Nurse Brown ignores me and turns to the others. "I have some news," she says.

"I know what it is! The kitchen quit because they don't feel their talents are being appreciated. And they have gone to cook for the Humane Society," I say.

"Poor dogs," Lily says, and shakes her head.

Nurse Brown clears her throat. "About the noise . . ."

"What noise?" I yell over the hammering.

"MARTY, SHUT UP!" Nurse Brown explodes.

Everybody jumps. Rose, always the last to finish eating, stabs her cheek with a spoonful of slop. She had used ketchup as cover-up for her eggs, but now she is wearing it as blush. I stifle a flinch and raise my eyebrows at Nurse Brown. I take out my imaginary chart and my pretend pen and make some notes about her little outburst. I mumble my observations, "Something's crawled up Madame's butt."

"What's that?"

"I heard Madonna was a slut. But I don't believe it," I say, nice and loud.

There are a couple of nervous giggles. Nervous because Brown is different today. And they're not sure whose side it's safer to be on.

"That's enough," she says, calm again.

They pick sides. The room is silent.

"Marty, I'm not going to do this with you today. I'm going to make my announcement uninterrupted."

Hammering begins.

"The noise you hear is coming from the group therapy room," Brown yells.

Right on cue, the noise stops. *These guys are good. Maybe they're former patients.*

Nurse Brown adjusts her volume and continues, "We are renovating the group therapy room to accommodate a library and some new, more comfortable furniture. So, for the next three days, you will have GT here in the dining hall." Nurse Brown looks around like she was expecting a cheer. "Rhonda is going to be delayed. She is counseling a new patient."

New patient. Fresh bones.

"You can do your bathroom break in here."

Let's see. That's ten girls. Taking ten minutes each to dissect ourselves in the mirror. To see where breakfast went today. Oatmeal to the backs of the arms, cottage cheese to the butt, butter to the belly, toast to the thighs, eggs to the ankles.

"Why can't we go to our rooms?"

"I don't want you girls wandering around. The staff is a little tied up right now."

What don't you want us to see? Maybe the staff is tied up tying the new girl down. Aye, Marty, could be we've got a fighter on our hands.

"Why don't you all play a game? The games are in the cupboard beside you, Marty."

World's Smallest Murder Weapon Found Missing

"I don't believe it." I search the box for the third time. They are definitely not here. I start to laugh.

Jamie comes over to investigate. "Hey, is that CLUE?"

"*Duh!*"

"I used to have one."

"A clue? Really? I can't picture you with one."

"Ha-ha-ha. I had the game, stupid. . . . Where are all the pieces?"

"That's what cracked me up. I think the assholes with the nametags took them . . . for our own safety, of course."

Katherine starts to laugh and says, "Probably thought we would bash ourselves with the candlestick."

Victoria smiles and giggles, "Or hang ourselves with the little plastic rope."

Elizabeth yells from the bathroom, "Or slash our wrists with the knife."

"Or blow our brains out with the world's smallest revolver," I add.

"We could be fierce figure skaters and whack each other on the shins with the lead pipe," Nancy says, and demonstrates by hitting Bonnie with a toothpick.

Bonnie jumps up and hops around the room yelling, "Why me?"

One by one we *all* start laughing. We are so hungry for fat laughs, we're like sharks in a feeding frenzy chasing tuna. You never realize how hungry you are till you take the first bite.

Jamie is the first to come up for air. "Maybe they thought we would shove Miss Scarlet and Professor Peacock up our noses and they would suffocate us." She laughs and snorts so hard that if she had a game piece up her nose, it would have shot up into her brain. Maybe they had a point.

Lily squeals, "The wrench! We forgot the wrench!" and points to something that Catwoman is holding.

The laughing stops.

Catwoman's left hand rests on top of the table. In her palm is a tiny perfect wrench made out of tinfoil. While we were laughing, Catwoman had been busy making weapons.

Katherine says, "We could hit Nurse Brown on the back of the head, but all that would do is give her a black eye."

We all lose it. Again. Even Catwoman looks like she's smiling.

Everybody starts checking the garbage cans and picking out the little silver thermal blankets that had covered our breakfasts.

"SPAGHETTI!" Victoria cries.

"What?" I say.

"Spaghetti! I'll use some from dinner tonight."

"For what?"

"The ROPE! If I lay one piece in figure eights on top and wrap it twice around the middle and let it dry, we'll have the rope. It'll even be the same color."

"NO!" someone outside our little workshop yells.

All the elves stop. All eyes ask the same question. *New girl?*

Nurse Brown comes in and knocks on the door to get our attention. We ignore her. She pulls a rubber glove over her hand and snaps it on her wrist. It works better than the door thing. "Okay. There will be no group therapy this morning. Rhonda is still busy with the new patient. And I will be too."

A feeding tube is draped around her neck.

"If anybody needs anything, you can ask Nurse Jane. Lunch will be at 12:00 as usual," Nurse Brown says and leaves.

Whoever the new girl is, if she's joining us for lunch, she won't be needing silverware.

It's a Guy Thing

"It's a WHAT?" *This can't be true. Katherine's just messing with me.*

"A guy." Katherine is flopped on her bed changing her nail polish for the third time today.

"No way."

"Yes way. I saw the hair on his arms."

"So what? We all had that baby-hair-suit when we came in."

"His was darker and thicker."

"Maybe she's just gorilla girl."

"That's not nice," Katherine says.

"I'm not trying to be nice. I'm being scientific. Maybe he's an it."

"Why does it bother you so much that the new patient is male?"

"What are you? My psychiatrist!"

"No. It's just . . . I don't get it."

"I don't want a guy in here. I just don't."

The Visit

"Knock, knock." I try to sound cheerful.

No answer from the corpse. He's lying on his back with the sheet folded up to his collarbone, exposing naked, pointed shoulders. Tubes going in and out of the holes in his body. You would think he's an organ donor. Except that he's been eating his heart, liver, and kidneys for months. So he bites as a savior. But he looks like Christ in his shroud of white linen. So still.

Silently I walk up to him. I've learned how to keep the tiles from talking. I put two fingers on his upturned wrist.

"What are you doing?" he cries, sitting up.

"Checking for a pulse." I try to keep my voice steady. But he is freaking me out. Yellow eyes behind stringy long hair. His nose starts to bleed from his sudden movement.

Freak. Freak. Freak. I want to run and cry and throw up and cry. And then vomit.

But I don't.

Breathe. Just breathe. Soundlessly. Drop your shoulders just like they taught you. Show no fear. You can take this guy. Do something different. Do something normal.

"What's your name?" I ask.

No answer. He tilts his head back and opens his mouth slightly, as if he's going to lick the blood crawling onto his upper lip. Instead he drops his chin. Closes his mouth.

And lets the blood continue onto his bottom lip, into the cleft in his chin, and finally one drop falls into his lap on the white sheet. I remember when I was so hungry, I'd suck the blood out of my own cuts. But not this guy. He won't even allow himself to recycle.

He lies back. I can see up his nose and the glob of coagulation stuff that has closed his wound. He stares with unfocused eyes up at the ceiling. I used to do that. That shit used to drive everyone crazy . . . it's driving me crazy. Crazy angry crazy.

I stomp out loudly. Try to slam the door behind me. But it's rigged so it won't shut. Takes me two tries to figure this out. Only the chain at the top of the door rattles. The nurse at the nurses' station jerks her head up at the noise. I head for her.

"Is he alright, Marty?"

"Yeah. I fixed him. He wants a pizza and a chocolate shake."

"Really?" the nurse asks.

"What do you think?" But I realize her "really?" isn't a stupid question. Just a desperate one.

"Did he talk to you?"

"No."

The nurse shakes her head and exhales. They never do this. Especially in front of patients. I wouldn't want her job. I try to think of something to say. The best I can do is, "Why don't you put him in the psych ward for a while? It worked for me."

The nurse lets her face leak a small smile.

"What's his name anyways?"

"Chris."
Figures.

Dr. Marty

I go to the "library," formally known as the group therapy room. It will always be the GT room. The group torture chamber, no matter how they dress it up.

The door is gone. And the doorjambs have been ripped off, taking paint and pieces of the wall with them. A gaping chapped-lipped hole. New, heavy square chairs wrapped in thick plastic line the walls to make a semicircle. At the back of the room, by the window, sits one unwrapped chair. It's black. No, it's blue. Blue leather. Hard to see the color because of the glare from the frosted windows.

I walk in and sit in the chair. It barely mumbles. Its blue skin is cold. I rub its arms. The smooth ride of my palm hits some rough spots. I lean over to look. I see dark blue with pale blue scratches on its arms, like the chair had tried to slit its wrists. I laugh when I figure out the real reason for the marks.

Rhonda pokes her head into the room. "What's so funny?"

"The chairs were too fat to fit through the door."

"That's what's so funny?"

"In here, it's hysterical."

"Yeah, I see why you would think so," Rhonda says and goes to one of the plastic bagged chairs and flops into it like a stuntman landing on a crash pad. She sinks as the air escapes, making her look like she's getting smaller. "Where is everyone?"

"They're in bugging what's-his-name," I say, picking at the scraped leather.

"Chris. And you've met him, haven't you?" Rhonda says, looking at me.

"Yeah. He's a real talker. Couldn't get him to shut up."

Rhonda does her eyebrow thing.

"How old is he?" I ask.

"Eighteen."

"God. He looks ancient. Like he's thirty . . . more like thirty-three."

"That old, huh?" Rhonda laughs.

"What's he doing here?"

"You're too smart to ask stupid questions," Rhonda says seriously.

"How long has he got?" I look at my feet.

"Who knows? A week, maybe more. The human body is an amazing thing. You guys hate it, starve it, and torture it, and it keeps on struggling to survive."

Images of POW's invade my head.

"Care to come back to the conversation, or do you want to stay in your head for a while?" Rhonda asks.

"I was just thinking."

"Do you ever do that? Just think? Somehow I imagine your thoughts entering like air into one of those long straight balloons. But then you turn it and twist it into some kind of animal and then you paint it black and white. . . ."

You should try letting the balloon float around for a while. Maybe even leave it pink."

"Two and a half questions, Rhonda."

Rhonda nods. "Okay."

"One. Are you calling me an airhead? Two. What are you smoking and can I have half?"

"No. Nothing and no," Rhonda says, and laughs.

"Where are the parents?"

"Whose?"

"Chris's."

"At home, I guess."

"Hiding behind the newspaper and the stock market and fresh squeezed orange juice."

"You think you've got his story all figured out." Rhonda sits up.

"What?"

"Not everyone who comes here has shitty parents."

"But Chris's, they're not coming, are they? Even though he's dying."

"His kidneys have basically shut down and he refuses dialysis," Rhonda says, just stating the facts in the same tone she'd use to report we were out of cereal.

"Jerk."

"Katherine said his being here upset you. Why?" Rhonda turns her head in my direction.

"Why can't she keep her mouth shut?" I say, and get *the look*. "He pisses me off."

"Every guy who comes in here makes you mad. I still haven't figured that one out, but can you tell me why Chris sets you off?" Rhonda tries not to beg.

"If I tell you, will you promise not to hit me with it in group?"

"Okay."

I don't know if this is the right thing to do. Telling the truth. To *staff*. But I like Rhonda. At least she has a sense of humor and does what she says she'll do. Or won't do. *There is always Plan B. If she uses this against me, I can always kill myself.*

I take a deep breath. "All my life I've played against the boys. I didn't like to lose and they didn't appreciate when I won. Not eating was a sport I didn't have to compete in with them. The one thing I would always be better at. Anorexia is for girls."

"And?"

"And now this guy comes in and he has beaten all of us. He had to one-up us."

"That is really warped."

"I know." *Well, I didn't know it till I said it out loud.*

Rhonda wipes at her eyes like I just threw sand in them. "Do you all think like this?" she says, and starts to massage her temples.

"I only know what *I* think. We don't talk to each other the way you think we do. We're too busy competing."

"Do you honestly think Chris came into this unit to beat the girls at their own game?"

"No."

"And by not eating, what do you think he's gaining . . . I mean winning?"

"Nothing. But those girls are in his room right now, aren't they? At his feet and at his side, moving his greasy hair out of his eyes with their fingertips. Begging him to eat. It's worse than a soap opera. . . . And he doesn't even appreciate it."

"Why doesn't he appreciate it?"

"They're not the ones he wants."

"Who do you think he wants?"

"His father. To come down here and save him. So he can say, 'It's too late. See what you did to me? Go to hell!'"

"How do you know this?"

"I just know . . . don't push it," I say and try to lift my hands from the chair arms. But I have to peal them off the leather. I can see the fingertip dents I've caused. Rhonda looks at the sweaty little bruises. Then at me. I put my hands behind my head and stare up at the ceiling. Out of the corner of my eye, I see Rhonda do the same.

She says, "So, what do you think of the new room?"

"I think if blue chairs and blue walls and blue Valium is all this place has got to offer, then we're all going to end up like Chris, who is going to end up like one of these chairs – a blue piece of skin covered in plastic with a tag around one foot."

Too Nice to Die

I stickhandle the food around my plate like a hockey player does a puck. I haven't talked to anyone in days. They haven't even noticed.

"I feel sorry for him. I think he's really nice," Rose says.

Nobody asks who she's talking about. There's only one *him*.

"How do you know he's nice, Rose? Did you talk to him?" I bark and break my silence.

"No."

"Did he talk to you?"

"No."

"Then how do you know?"

"He doesn't deserve to die."

"NONE OF US DESERVES TO DIE!" I shout, and stand up so fast my chair goes flying and slams into the wall. I almost bump into Nurse Brown, who meets me in the doorway and blocks my escape. I close my eyes and prepare for battle. "I'm going to see Jackie."

"Okay," Brown says and moves out of the doorway.

I look over at her. "Excuse me?"

"I'll call down to her office and let her know you're coming, if that's alright with you?"

"Ahh . . . yeah . . . thanks." I walk towards the elevator, but I keep looking back. Waiting for Nurse Brown to pop out from behind the station and yell, "Psych!" Nobody pops or yells anything. I get on the elevator alone and take it down to the basement, where I hope Jackie is waiting for me. It seems a shorter walk to Jackie's office than I remember.

"Knock, knock!" I say, and tap on the door with my knuckles.

No answer. I put my ear against the wood and listen for little psychologist-at-work noises.

Nothing.

No creaking of a chair or scuffing of feet. No crying followed by Kleenexes being ripped from their cozy little home. Nothing but regular silence.

So, Marty, what do you want to do now?

I stand against the wall facing the door. *Jackie should be here soon.* When she didn't answer her office phone, Nurse Brown would've paged Jackie. They are not going to let me be alone anywhere for long.

Might as well have seat. Sitting here is better than going back upstairs. Just the thought of it makes me mad again. I never got one ounce of sympathy from them. And I never saw them feel sorry for themselves.

The door of Jackie's office opens. I don't look up. I have a staring contest with her shoes. I win. The shoes go back to hiding under her desk. I go into the office. Sit in the usual chair. No blue leather loungers for Jackie's office. You're not supposed to be comfortable down here.

"So was that supposed to be some kind of psychologist's joke . . . or maybe a test?" I ask.

"To tell you the truth, when Nurse Brown called me I opened the door immediately. But then I thought maybe

I'd see what would happen if you thought I wasn't here."

"So how did I do? How's my frustration tolerance these days?"

"A lot better than before."

She's right. Before, I would have kicked the door or punched the wall. Or both.

"But Nurse Brown did mention that you were abusing chairs."

"Just so I don't lose any brownie points, the chair fell when I stood up."

"Why?"

"Damn it, Jackie, the *whys* drive me nuts. And so do the other girls."

Jackie doesn't say anything.

"I can't take them anymore. This crap about how Chris doesn't deserve to die. But they can't apply that fact to themselves. They pray every night to protect other people and ask God if maybe he had some time, could he help them. It's crap and it's boring and God's never in his office. Their parents don't come. Nobody is coming."

"Your parents came."

"Yes, they . . . yes, they did."

"Your mom comes all the time. She would see you more but it seems to upset you, and she says she doesn't want to do that. She goes to the support meetings twice a week. Your dad came from New York . . ."

"Because he was in LA," I counter.

"He still came, Marty. Some of these parents are twenty minutes away and they don't visit. Yours are different."

"Don't tell me I'm lucky." I laugh.

"Not lucky, just different . . . maybe different enough to help you leave here and make it in the real world."

"Yeah. The real world is just begging me to join it."

"It would if you were to be something other than anorexic."

"I don't know how to be anything else." I look at the floor.

"What were you before?"

"I don't know – I can't remember."

"I can get your records, if you really can't remember."

"I failed at all of those things," I say, looking up at her.

"No, you didn't. You quit. You didn't get the attention you needed, so you went on to something else. There is a big difference between failing and quitting," Jackie says, staring back.

"I haven't even finished high school."

"Neither did I." Jackie smiles.

"So I'm being counseled by a high school dropout?"

"I didn't get my high school diploma till I was twenty-one," she says.

"Must have been weird going back to school at that age."

"Actually, I didn't go back to class. I had this amazing English teacher, Mr. MacLeod. My mother wrote to him to ask if I could finish the papers I needed to graduate and would he mark them. He sent the assignments to me. I did the papers and sent them back. He never asked why I didn't call him myself, or why I didn't do it earlier. . . . He just helped me. I learned a lot about not judging people from him."

"Are you saying I judge people?" I ask.

"We all do, Marty. But we use different standards. You expect yourself and everyone around you to be perfect."

"You want to know why? I'll tell you. My parents prefer picture-perfect. No mess. No fuss. Just get the job done."

"You can only expect people – and parents are people too – to do what they can do. And sometimes it's not much. But if you expect any more than that, you are always going to get shafted. Always."

"Have you given my parents that little speech?"

"What does it matter? You can't control what *they* do. Only what *you* do."

"Well, it feels like I don't know how to do anything . . . right."

"Is right the same as perfect?"

"I don't know."

"I know something you do well," Jackie says, sitting up straighter in her chair. "Art. What's great about art is that it is subjective. You can only judge it by what you like and what you don't. There is no perfect."

"An anorexic artist – that's perfect." I laugh.

Jackie doesn't look impressed, but she begins to smile.

"I'm just kidding, Jack," I say, leaning forward a little.

"I know you are, and that's why I'm going to make you an offer. How about teaching art to kids?"

A pause. "Are you joking?"

"No. I have a friend who runs the community center across from the art college downtown."

"And?"

"And she needs people to work with kids at the center."

"Do you not like children, Jackie?"

"I like them best of all. Adults and anorexics are a pain in the ass. But it pays the bills." She laughs.

"I'm serious. You would really inflict me upon innocent children?"

"Look, I see the way you are with Lily. I've seen your paintings. I'm putting myself on the line, but I'm willing to. Because I believe in you. Do you?"

"I believe I'll think about it."

DAY 107
SEPTEMBER 28

Smog Alert

Code blue.

From my room I see Chris's parents for the first time. I watch Chris's mother watch the staff work on her son.

I go to the window.

His father is waiting out in the car.

The motor is running.

Rose Garden

After group therapy on Wednesdays, we get a ten-minute break, return to the GT room, and make the list for the Friday meal.

"Marty, would you mind locating Rose and letting her know we are about to start?" Nurse Brown asks.

"I . . ." *Hold your tongue, Marty; this little assignment gets you out of the room.* "Yeah, sure. It might take me a while to find her."

"Rose is in the garden."

Of course she is. Where she always is when it's time to make the list.

"You can go now, Marty," Brown says.

I can taste the envy in the air. Even temporary escapes are considered delicacies. I leave the GT room and head for the garden. I walk down the hall on the twenty squares of blue carpet it takes to get me to the door with careful glass diamonds that allow me to look safely on the garden.

The Garden. What a joke. Big square cement patio slabs. With lots of crisscross cracks to break our mothers' backs. And there is Rose. Stomping on all the lines. Lifting her knees up past her waist to get maximum thrust on the way down. When the half-barrel planter with the limp pansies and dried-up marigolds gets in her way, she goes around it. Several times. It's a small garden. The far corners are very near. Fence in our secrets. The "green space" has dead-man's gray walls and a jaundice yellow floor. And there is Rose, all red from her efforts and the sun.

I open the door and say, "The list."

Rose stops hurting her mother for a moment. "Shit," she says.

The List

"Whose turn is it to write down the list?" Nurse Brown says.

No one answers. Everyone freezes in their chairs.

She has asked that every Wednesday for four months. The same words in the same tone. From the same chair. I wouldn't be surprised if there was a tape recorder in the arm of the chair – she sits, presses PLAY, and moves her lips. She gets the same answer. Every week.

"Rose, I think it's your turn," Brown says.

Nobody knows whose turn it really is. Nobody wants a turn at writing the grocery list. Brown passes one of two notepads to Rose and throws her a pen. Nurse Brown always writes down the list too. Ever since the day it was Jamie's turn. Jamie's pad had THINGS TO DO written across the top. It took one hour and thirty-seven minutes to make up the list the day it was Jamie's turn to write it. And at the end of the one hour and thirty-seven minutes (not a record), it was discovered that under THINGS TO DO Jamie had written: **killmyself.**

Forty-three times.

"Whose turn is it to decide what this week's Friday meal will be?" Nurse Brown asks. Her second rhetorical question of the day.

Everyone shrinks back a little. We stop breathing.

Nurse Brown takes a deep breath . . .

And the winner is . . .

Nurse Brown exhales, "Marty, I believe you deserve the honor."

Everyone exhales, except me. *Shit.* "What did *I* do?"

"Nothing . . . you make deciding the meal sound like a punishment."

It *is* a punishment. There is no menu to choose from. It's hard enough to get ten normal eating people to decide what to have for dinner. Try making that decision for ten of us. Some won't eat bread or any carbohydrates. Some won't eat anything with sugar in it, including tomato sauce. Some won't eat any dairy because those darn cows make grass into fat. And *everyone* won't eat FAT.

You cannot cannot cannot make anyone happy. Which means, you'll never be a hero. Only an old goat. Until next Wednesday, when Nurse Brown picks a new goat.

"Turkey. Thanksgiving turkey dinner." It just flies out of my mouth.

And the chicken coop goes nuts. They start flapping their little, bony, flaky, dried-up wings and squawking about mashed potatoes need butter, gravy is disgusting, there is sugar in cranberry sauce. Lots. Did you know that? There is sugar and butter in everything. The people who make frozen turkeys probably make the turkeys eat sugar cubes and force them to drink butter. Like the cigarette companies put extra stuff in cigarettes to make them more addictive. Carrots are okay. We all agree on carrots. They're the only thing we agree on. Every Wednesday. They are first on the list.

When the feathers settle, Nurse Brown looks at me and says, "Why turkey, Marty?"

"Why not?"

"I'm just surprised. Thanksgiving dinner is a very family meal."

"Not in my family."

"What is Thanksgiving about then?"

"It has to do with Indians, who didn't know what they were getting themselves into, and with turkeys, ripe and practicing for Christmas because 'You're going to miss it 'cause you'll be with your dad this year' and it's the single biggest weekend of the year for retail. And it's for my mother to swear at the gravy and give thanks to God for making the grandmothers deaf, so they can't hear the electric can opener."

Nurse Brown doesn't ask me any more questions. She drums her fingers on the notepad and says, "Okay, let's start our list."

The evil eye campaign starts again. I'm sick of being grilled. "I could change my mind to luau – roast a nice fat piggy in the parking lot?"

Elizabeth squeals.

But I don't change my mind about the turkey. Because they are expensive and take an ice age to thaw out, so you only get one shot at it, but it's a pretty narrow one, so it's real easy to fuck up. Fuck is my mother's favorite Thanksgiving word.

The Grocery Store

Nobody is talking to me. *Like it's my idea to come here and pick up the things on the list.* The brain trusts back at Silver Lake think that if we hang out in the place where all the food lives, then we will get used to it. *Fat chance.* The B's walk through the store like reformed gamblers through a casino: they stare at the ice-cream freezer as if it were a roulette wheel. Until Rhonda drags them away. The A's are walking down the very middle of the aisles lined with food like people afraid of puppies would move through Humane Society kennels packed with junkyard dogs. The A's would turn sideways, and walk that way, if Rhonda wasn't pushing them to the back of the store.

Rhonda herds us into a corner, right in front of the refrigerated deli case with all the bacon and hot dogs and every water-retaining sodium-packed product known to man. We school like fish for protection. Try to get into the middle of the group and sacrifice our buddies to the outside. Where the bacon is. Rhonda does a head count to make sure none of the fish got away.

"I don't see Jamie. Does anyone know where Jamie is?" she asks.

Nobody knows. *Of course.*

"Marty, will you go find her, please?"

130

"Why do *I* always get sent to get people?"

"Because you bring them back."

"Fine." *Not fine, but it's better than a group search, which would mean we'd be in this grocery store all day.*

I know where to find Jamie. I walk to the junk food aisle. If the other customers knew where we were from, they would think that Jamie was an anorexic. She's not. She's a bony bulimic. I find her. She's having a staring contest with an economy-size bag of barbeque potato chips.

"Long lost friend?" It's a mean thing to say, but I'm pissed.

No answer. Not even a flinch or dirty look. This is not like Jamie.

"Rhonda wants you to —"

"I used to eat three of these in one day," Jamie says, and reaches out with both hands and picks up the bag. She holds it gently around the waist. "I'd go to a store to buy some carrots. Did you ever notice that the fruit and vegetables are on one side of grocery stores and the shit food is on the other?" she says, still looking at the bag.

I don't know if she's talking to the chips or me. Neither one of us answers.

"I'd come into the store for some carrots. You know, something healthy. Every time I'd come for the carrots, I'd test myself and come to this aisle. To reward myself for not buying ice cream, I'd pick a small bag of chips. Since I picked the small bag, I figured I deserved some ice cream anyways. So I'd get a small container of vanilla. I don't really like vanilla, but it has the least number of calories. But you already know that," Jamie says to the chips, but

I'm sure she's talking to me. "Then I'd think, if I'm going to eat ice cream, I might as well have my favorite – double chocolate fudge chunk. And I didn't want to come back to the store for a long time, so I'd grab the family-size fudge chunk. Then I'd know I was screwed, so I'd put the small bag of chips back. And grab three bags of these bastards," Jamie says. She gives the huge bag of chips a violent shake. Then hugs it to her chest like a pillow. Hugs it hard. Till it explodes. It sounds like a gunshot. When the red smoke clears, she lets the bag fall to the floor and brushes barbeque powder from her chin and shirt. "Let's go."

As we leave, a store manager rounds the corner. He looks confused.

As we pass him, I say, "Cleanup in the aisle of evil."

Jamie smiles. Her yellow teeth explain how she can eat so much and stay so thin.

We're Back

"Where have you guys been?" Rhonda says, annoyed.

"I was looking for carrots," Jamie says.

Rhonda narrows her eyes. "Did you two have anything to do with that loud bang?"

"All bangs are loud, aren't they?" I'm a stickler for detail.

Rhonda gives me maximum glare.

It works. "Jamie killed a bag of chips."

"I don't want to know," Rhonda says, shakes her head and looks away.

That's the problem with the truth. Everyone wants it. They just don't want to know it.

The Turkey

We line the freezer single file and bend over like we would a railing on a bridge, but we're looking for turkeys instead of fish. Everybody scans the tags of the dead birds for numbers. Not price numbers. Because money is no object. We look for weight numbers. Our obsession. We have to have a pound and a half per person. Ten of us (unless someone croaks, or their insurance runs out) plus two staff equals eighteen pounds of dead frozen bird.

Rhonda starts picking up birds from the freezer, checking the tags, and then putting them back. Tag and release. Tag and release. Until she has a pile of birds that weigh around eighteen pounds.

Rhonda steps away from the freezer. She has narrowed it down to five candidates. It is up to us to make the final selection as to who will be Miss Thanksgiving.

The debate begins.

"This one's 18.23," Victoria says.

"But it's butter basted," Rose whines.

"I didn't see that," Victoria protests.

"Yeah, right," Rose responds.

"Screw you," Victoria finishes.

Turkey number 18.23 is not a contender because she has too much fat.

"This one is 18.17. Nonbasted." Katherine takes the floor.

"It's stuffed," Jamie states.

"So? Then we won't have to make stuffing," Katherine argues.

"Ready-made stuffing has a shit load of sodium. Bloat factor is too high," Jamie expounds.

"That's not good," Katherine agrees.

Contestant number 18.17 is out for retaining too much water.

"Here. No butter. No stuffing. 18.11," Nancy says like she thinks she's found the winner.

"I read in the paper that this company uses hormones to make their turkeys grow faster," Elizabeth informs.

18.11 is immediately disqualified and should be sent for drug testing.

Catwoman picks up a bird and stares at it. She carries it to the freezer with the boxes of chicken nuggets and drops it in.

Lily goes over to see. "18.06, but it's a goose."

18.06 is ineligible for pretending to be something it's not.

Bonnie says, "You pick, Marty. It's your meal."

I choose an organic free-range Cornish hen. It weighs .18 pounds. I'm dyslexic. Everyone votes for the Cornish girl.

"For Christ's sake, Marty!" Rhonda says, and picks the last one of the five. We have our winner. 18.03. But she is not the crowd favorite.

The Cornish hen is still number one in our hearts. I bowl her down the freezer into the pile of runner-ups. She takes a bounce and ends up on top anyways. Bonnie crowns her with a can of tuna.

Next stop on the tour – sour cream.

Oops

We bring the bird home. I'm last out of the bus, so I have to carry it inside. The bird is double bagged, but with the cheap plastic bags that look like rice paper. So I carry it from the bottom. And along the bottom of the bags, I run my ragged nails. I've chewed them so much they are serrated like steak knives. As we approach the entrance, they cut through the bags like magic. The bags release the bird into the world. It's a rough start. The turkey bounces down seventeen stairs, hits the walkway, leaps onto the tarmac, and slides across the parking lot till it stops right under the bus's bum. The bus looks like it has laid an egg.

"I think it wants a ride back to the store," I say to Rhonda.

"Drop it again and I'll go get some ducks for dinner."

Ducks are about 210% fat. I used to eat duck. I still like it. I just won't eat it.

I go and pull the turkey out from under the bus and carry it to the unit kitchen. Carefully.

Too Many Cooks

Friday, 9:00 A.M.

"You pull it out," Rose says.

"You pull it out," I say.

"I'll pull it out," Lily says.

"That's okay, Lil, I'll get it out. It weighs more than you do," I say.

Lily opens the door to the fridge. On the bottom shelf lies the turkey. I slide it out on its silver tray like a body from the morgue.

"Now what do we do?" asks Lily.

"I don't know." And I don't. Mom's never let me touch one.

"I do," Jamie says from the doorway. She walks to the counter and talks at the bird. "My mom loves Thanksgiving. She always cooks two birds and two pots of everything. She could never figure out where the leftovers went. Until she found them undigested in the toilet I clogged up." Jamie turns to me. "It's supposed to go tits up."

"It already did that," I say.

"In the oven, idiot," Jamie says.

"I don't see any boobs on this bird," I say.

"Maybe it's flat-chested," Lily says, and looks down at her shirt.

Jamie turns the bird over a couple of times and says, "This side up."

The top of the turkey is dented and its skin is split. I had almost given it a mastectomy when I dropped it down the stairs.

"Now you have to grease it up," instructs Chef Jamie.

We play rock, paper, scissors to see who has to give the bird a butter massage.

Rose loses. She does the fastest lube job in the history of cooking.

I turn the oven to 500 degrees because that is as high as it will go. "Lily, get away from the stove; it's going to get very hot." I start to shove the bird in the oven and realize too late that the rack is too high. The tray goes in, but the top of the oven stops the turkey. It squirts through my arms, hits the oven door, and shoots through my legs like a puck through a goalie's five hole.

"How many times are you going to send that turkey for a ride?" Jamie smiles.

"Shut up, Jamie . . . where did it go?"

"It flew past me. I think it's out in the hall," Lily says.

I look from the oven to the kitchen doorway. The flight path is clearly marked by a dull trail of butter along the glossy floor. Lily is right. The turkey must have set a land-speed record on linoleum before it hit the hall. The carpet stopped it cold. If the bird had a neck, it would have gotten whiplash.

I try to pick up the turkey, but it's like trying to grab a greased pig. "Would somebody help me . . . please?"

Jamie comes over. She is still smirking. "What do you want me to do?"

"Help me lift this thing. . . . Rose, you bring the tray over." Rose gets the potholders and retrieves the pre-heated tray from the oven. "Okay, Jamie and I are going to lift the turkey and you slide the tray underneath it . . . just like in those hospital emergency shows. On my count, ready? One, two, three!"

Lily walks beside the body as we transport it to the counter. She examines it closely and reports, "There's dirt and carpet fuzz on it."

"Don't worry, Lil, it'll burn off. Nobody is going to eat the skin anyway." I move the oven rack down and load the turkey. "Rhonda said it has to cook for about six hours, so I won't have to look at it again till 3:30."

"Who's going to baste it?" Jamie asks.

"Don't know and don't care," I say, washing my hands of butter and bird juice while Jamie licks her fingers clean. "Aren't you worried about getting sick?"

"So I throw up and have diarrhea for three days? Big deal. It'd be just like old times," Jamie says and smiles.

I want out of this kitchen. It's hot and close. And ever since the chip thing at the store, Jamie keeps throwing more-than-I-want-to-know curveballs at me. And they are starting to hit home.

Does she know I used to throw up too? That I'm not a pure A? That I'm a combination A and B? I'm a mutt. And you know what they do with mutts, Marty. They put them down.

I need an excuse to leave. "Come on, Lily, let's go draw a turkey centerpiece."

We leave Rose and Jamie to guard the bird to make sure it doesn't get away. Again.

That's a Stupid Place to Put It

Rhonda comes into the staff "cottage" that the alchies and druggies use, across the yard. The cottage looks like someone converted a garage into one big kitchen and dining room. She looks over Lily's shoulder. "That's nice, Lily. It'll look pretty on the table."

"It was Marty's idea."

"Really?" Rhonda says, and up goes her left eyebrow.

"Yes, really," I say. "I thought something festive for the table might be nice to go with the pilgrim hats and straight jackets."

Rhonda pretends she doesn't hear me. "Did you get the turkey in the oven?"

"Yes." *But it took a little side trip first.*

"What did you do with the gizzards?" Rhonda looks around.

"Lizards?" Lily makes a face.

"Not lizards, Lily, gizzards . . . where are they?"

"Where are they supposed to be?" I say.

"What are gizzards?" Lily asks.

"The kidneys, liver, and heart of the turkey. Some people use them to make the gravy. You did take them out, didn't you?"

"Out of where?"

"Marty, the *turkey*. That's what's in the little bag inside it."

"How the fuck was I supposed to know the stupid bird had carry-on luggage?" I stomp back to the kitchen. "Fuck." *This is beginning to feel like a real Thanksgiving.*

Dinner

Six girls in the kitchen cooking. Five girls bitching. Catwoman uncans the cranberry sauce in silence.

Rhonda comes in for the eighth time. "How's it going, girls?"

"Hey, Rhonda, how many anorexics does it take to stuff a turkey?" I ask.

Rhonda gives me the look. "Okay, how many?"

"I figure we could fit about three in this one," I say as I carry the turkey to her.

Rhonda carves the bird. None of us are allowed to play with knives.

We go to the dining room and sit down to dinner in silence.

"Let's say grace," Nurse Brown commands from the head of the table.

We bow our heads.

"Grace," Rhonda says from the other end.

They don't make us say grace. They can't force God down our throats, only food.

The B's gobble the turkey down.

The A's pick at it.

Rose gags on a piece. "It's too dry," she coughs.

Rhonda looks ready to blow. "Eat it, or I'll order pizza with double sausage and triple cheese."

The B's look sorry they ate theirs.

The A's eat faster.

Fifteen Minutes Later

Dinner is finished.

DAY 153
NOVEMBER 13

I Can't Talk While My Mouth Is Full

I'm on my bed. Mom breezes in.

"Hi, Marty."

"Hi, Mom."

Then nothing. Always the same. We go through the hi's and then we hit the lows. This dance we do so well.

"Zack has been asking again if he can come see you. I don't think it's a good idea, but it's up to you."

Nothing is ever up to me. Seventeen seconds into the visit and already something that concerns me isn't a good idea.

"Did you hear me, Marty?"

"Yes, Mom."

"What are you going to do?"

"I don't know."

"Well, I think calling him would be alright. I'll call him when I get home and let him know you are going to do that. Okay? OKAY, Marty?"

"YES, Mom. Whatever you want to do."

"It's not whatever *I want to do*. It just seems you're paralyzed and I'm doing this to help you . . . get you moving again. Zack is a terrific guy. It's too bad you two couldn't have met five years from now. You're so young, and sometimes I think you loved each other too much. You can love someone too hard you know."

Or not hard enough.

"Well, Marty, if you're not going to talk to me, then I guess I'll leave. I love you."

I love you, but I'm leaving and it's your fault.

"Good-bye, Marty."

Bye, Mom. I have a million words I need to say to you. So many they have dammed up my mouth. Lodged so tight, I'd need to spring a leak to speak.

I stay sitting on the bed, head down, eyes focused on my hands. On the scars left by all those words I couldn't say – the ones that had thrown themselves through windows and taken my fist with them.

Sticks and stones and broken glass can never hurt you . . . as much as words.

Show No Tear

"Marty, your father is on the phone," Katherine says and throws herself on my bed and bounces me off like some weird circus act.

Someone else to help me get moving.

"Did he say where he's calling from?" *Maybe . . . maybe.*

"Canada."

Maybe not.

I walk quickly past the nurses' station to the patients' phone. The suspense is over. Canada is a long way from California.

"Hi, Dad."

"Marty."

"Katherine said you're in Canada."

"Yes, but there's no snow."

"None here either."

"Ah, yeah. I guess there wouldn't be. I was just thinking about the last time we were here together. To see your grandmother at Christmas – there was a ton of snow then."

"Yeah, I remember." *But not much else, except a lot of food I wanted to eat so bad but didn't. Being so tired and brain starved, I kept lighting the wrong ends of cigarettes. Grandma's sad face when she looked into mine.* "We had a great time."

"Well, maybe we could do it again this coming Christmas. Your grandmother would love that."

"Sure, Dad." *I don't know what I'm doing tomorrow, but Christmas is covered.*

"Look, Marty, I called to say hi and let you know that I talked to your mother this morning and she said Zack has been asking to see you."

Suddenly it's a lot colder on the other end of the phone.

"Mom was just here. She told me . . ."

"I don't want you seeing him, Marty. I don't even want you to talk to him."

I don't make a sound. Can't afford to. If he hears or smells tears, he'll think I'm weak. Accuse me of crying to get out of something. I hold the receiver to my ear, but away from my mouth, so the salt water from my eyes and nose can splash onto my shoes. I can't breathe through my nose, can't snort the stuff back up it. So I breathe through my mouth. Saliva collects inside my cheeks, slides over my lips. I'm like a three stream fountain – a very quiet fountain.

All is quiet in Canada too. Two minutes go by. Four. And finally the dial tone.

Sex

I've been summoned to Jackie's office.

"Okay, Jackie, what did I do now?" I say, picking at the bald spot on the arm of the chair.

"Why do you think you did something, Marty?" Jackie says, leaning forward.

"Because you called me down and my next appointment isn't until Thursday."

144

"You didn't do anything."

"Well, somebody did, or I wouldn't be here."

"Your mother called," Jackie says, and leans back.

"Bingo." I raise my arms above my head.

"And your father."

"Bonus bingo."

"And Zack, but I didn't talk to him."

I drop my arms and bang my elbow. "Fucking jackpot." *Why is Zack calling Jackie? How does he know about her? And how did he get her number?*

"Marty? You with me?" Jackie opens a drawer and pulls out a pad of paper.

"Yeah. I know what my parents called about. You going to tell me what to do about Zack?"

"No, I'm asking what you would like to do."

"That's a novel idea."

"Well?"

"Well what, Jackie? It doesn't matter what I want to do. They never ask me. They just tell me what to do. It's easier on everyone if I just do it."

"You're talking about your parents?" Jackie makes a note.

"No. The gods of Mount Olympus. Did Zack leave a message?"

"Does Zack tell you what to do?"

"Everyone does. That's just life."

"It's not my life."

"Lucky you."

"Do you love Zack?" Jackie asks, putting down her pen.

Jackie's question is like the pop fly ball you stand in the middle of a big field to catch. You hear the ball leave the bat. It goes up till it disappears, but you know it's still there. You have to get underneath it just right. Because then it rockets down, and if you screw up, it will smash you in the face. Saving face has nothing to do with honor – it's the prize you get for catching those pop fly questions.

"Yes . . ." *I think so.* I catch the ball, but then let it roll out of the glove. *I don't want to lie to Jackie. But it's hard to tell the truth when you're not sure what the truth is.*

"Did you make love with him?"

"It was my decision . . ." *Sort of. Make love – what a stupid phrase. They should call it Trying to Get a Grip or See If You Can Do This and Breathe.*

That night with him. My body was screaming yes, acting like an octopus – exploring, sliding, gushing, wet. Never trust a body.

"Marty, making love is something people decide together."

"I've already had sex education, Jackie."

"And sex."

"So."

"So?"

"I've slept with more than one guy, you know." *There. Get it out. Give Jackie a nice grisly piece of meat to chew on.*

"And?" Jackie says. Swallows my guts whole and doesn't even make a face.

"And so, what do you think of me now?" I cross my arms.

"What do you think of yourself?" she throws back.

"Are you going to answer *any* of my questions?"

"Your answers are more important. But I'll give you mine. After. Okay?"

"Okay."

"So what do you think of you having sex with more than one guy?" Jackie looks at me.

"I think that makes me a slut." I look away.

"Why?"

"Because it does. If you have sex before you're eighteen, or before you're married, then you're a slut." *How the hell did we get here?*

"According to who?"

"My mother." *And how do I get out?*

"Your mom says you don't listen to anything she says, so why listen about sex?"

"Because if she knew she'd kill me."

"I can safely say she wouldn't kill you, Marty. She might be angry or upset, but I know your mother's situation. She just doesn't want you to make the same mistake she feels she made."

"That mistake being me. And if she hadn't had me, maybe she wouldn't have become an alcoholic." I cross my legs and kick the desk.

"Boy, you really screwed up as a baby."

"I know you're being sarcastic. You know I didn't even like it. I don't see why it's such a big deal and the rules stink."

"What rules?" Jackie asks.

"You know. You can't have sex without love. They won't love you if you don't have sex with them. Once you have sex with them, they can't love you anymore."

"Were you raped?"

"Not physically." My hands start to shake.

"How then?"

"Well, I'm pretty sure I said yes."

"If you said yes, then you had some control. If you said no, then you had no control. Do you think that would be fair to say?" She leans forward again.

"Whatever."

"What did you mean by 'not physically'?"

"I don't know." *I don't know why I told you all that stuff. So now you can put it in my chart, and they will all know I'm a slut. That I gave those guys what they wanted. Traded with them. My legs around them to have their arms around me. Let me think they would protect me, make everything alright, love me anyways.*

Love me. Not use me and only love the ones who say no. "Guys just want to kiss the no girl on the porch with the lights on for the world to see. Fuck the yes girl in the dark and tell the world what they missed."

"You sound angry."

"I am."

"Would you be a virgin again if you could?"

"Yes."

"Well, you can't."

"So what do I do?"

"Get over it."

"Thanks a lot, Jackie."

"I'll help you . . . I'm not going anywhere."

That's what they all say.

Christmas Present

I ignore the camera eyes. And walk to Jackie's office without a human escort. I feel like a little kid who gets to go to the store alone.

I make it safely and wave to the cameras. I almost expect them to acknowledge me with a nod. They don't. They just blink their red lights.

Jackie's door is open. She says it's always open, but that's not true. When Dad and I had our family session with her, she had locked it from the inside. I leave my feet in the hall and stick my head into the office.

"Come *all the way in*, hon. I just need to finish this up and I'll be right with you," Jackie says, without looking up. She waves me to a chair with one hand and continues writing with the other.

I'm impressed, so I take a seat and start patting the top of my head and rubbing my stomach in circles. I'm not very good at it.

"What are you doing?" Jackie puts down her pen and looks at me.

"Nothing, just trying to see if I can do two things at once."

"I bet you can do a million things at once – I bet that's what landed you in this place."

"You'd lose."

"Would I?"

"Yes. And I'm not up for this kind of crap today."

"What kind of crap are you up for then?"

I try the *I'm-tired-so-give-me-a-break* look.

"What about Christmas crap? You up for that?" Jackie asks cheerfully.

I don't know why I can't remember that this woman has no sympathy and shows no mercy. "What about Christmas?" I ask.

"It's two weeks away."

"So."

"So what do you want to do?"

"Celebrate Chanukah."

"I didn't know you were Jewish."

"I'm not."

"Well, I am."

"Then it must drive you nuts working with us pickers and pukers."

"Why would you think that?" Jackie says. Leans back into her chair and closes the door with her foot. Kicks her shoes under her desk.

Oh, God, she's going make me do time. I don't want to be here all day.

"Okay, Jack. I had a Jewish friend. I went over to her house."

"And . . ."

"And everything I've heard about Jews and food is true. Her mother wouldn't leave me alone. She kept pushing food at me. Saying, 'Eat! Eat!'"

"Did the mother do that every time you went there?"

"I only went once."

"Did you like this girl?"

"Yes."

"Then how come only once?"

And once again Jackie hits the right button. It's like her office is this memory machine. I hate this. But once Jackie puts you on the ride, it's impossible to get off.

I'm in the kitchen with Rachel and her mom. Then the grandmother walks in, looks at me, and screams. She covers her mouth to stop herself. Grabs a fistful of her blouse and rubs it back and forth across the washboard of her chest. She takes a shaking hand away from her mouth and asks Rachel's mother something in a language I've never heard. Rachel's mother answers in English, "She's not sick, Momma. She won't eat."

"I'm just dieting."

"Die – eating. That's a good idea. What's right is that you should DIE EATING. Not starving like this. You have no right to do such things. Such terrible things to the gift that God gave you."

I want to be mad at this woman. But she's mad enough for both of us. Mad and sad. She grabs my shoulders and digs in her fingers, like claws into a catch. But it's her eyes that hurt me. So much pain in the yellow whites and the red-rimmed eyelids, and a thousand tears that she won't let come. Because I don't deserve them.

"Stop it," she says.

*

"Marty? Can you tell me?" Jackie asks, and places the box of Kleenex in my lap.

I let it sit there. I refuse to use even one. *I'm Kleenorexic. I don't deserve the luxury that's in my lap.*

"Marty, I think it's enough for today . . . but maybe next week you'll tell me what happened?"

"Maybe."

"It could be your Christmas present to me."

"But you said you're Jewish."

"Yeah. . . . And I know a good deal when I see one."

Ghost of Christmas Pants

Mom's been here. Bed is remade. Edges are a little sharper than when I left it. If you licked them, you'd cut your tongue. At the end of the dangerous bed sits a stack of clean laundry. And buried in the middle is a pair of black preshrunk memories. The sweatpants my grandmother bought me last Christmas.

My heart bangs against my ribs. My lungs cower and refuse to move.

Stupid.

Just pants.

Yeah, right.

No such thing as just.

It must be theme day here at Camp Eat-a-Lot. Mom's in on it too. I don't know if she's brought the pants here to taunt me or haunt me. Either way it's working.

* .

Last Christmas was supposed to be perfect. Just like the Christmas before that and that and that and that. Except they weren't. Because every Christmas Mom got bombed and bombed and bombed and bombed. If there are some good bits about those Christmases, I don't remember them . . . because the ruins are so spectacular.

The black sweatpants are just one of the relics collected while out shopping with my grandmother. The airlines had lost her luggage. She wanted something for me. Something to put under our tree. The pathetic tree Mom had bought because she felt sorry for it. Some sort of tropical evergreen, whose branches were meant to sway in the breeze. They were too limp to hang ornaments on. Our tree couldn't hold up under the weight of Christmas, so we tied up its arms with fishing line. I was jealous of that stupid tree. It hogged all the sympathy and support. I had wished that someone would feel sorry for how limp I was. Had wanted my limbs to be held up by invisible threads of support. So when they hung things on me, I wouldn't feel like I was letting them down.

But it didn't happen that way.

As usual, the tree was a success. And I was a failure. I failed to want what Mom wanted.

"Get whatever you like," Grandma had said.

We were in front of a sports store. I went to the men's section and chose a pair of black sweatpants. Men's because they had a drawstring instead of an elastic waist. Black, to hide my fat ass. Big, so Mom wouldn't wear them. Wouldn't put them on and ask me if she looked fat.

"Why do you want those awful things?" Mom asked, *with that tone.*

"No reason, I just like them."

"They're huge. You'll look sloppy."

"They'll shrink," I said.

"At least get another color," Mom had ordered, without looking at me.

"Grandma said to get what I want." As soon as I said it, I knew it was a mistake. Mom had turned to me and leaned into my face and held me with her eyes. From her mouth, words dripped like venom.

"Why are you being so difficult? Do you know how much money has been spent on you already this Christmas? And you want black. Well, that's just perfect. Only bad girls wear black. Bad, dirty girls."

Just then Grandma came up to us, took the pants from me, and said, "Are these what you want, pumpkin? They look a little big."

"They fit her perfectly," Mom hissed, and then wove her way into the crowd until she disappeared.

Strike and leave.

My heart pounded and pumped the poison until I was paralyzed. Bile bubbled up through the small breathing hole left in my throat. I had to push everything down so I could breathe. Shove it down. Mash Mom's words like a garbage compacter and make them small. The size of a pill I could close my eyes and swallow.

Those words were more than I could chew. They still are.

*

Just as I'm throwing away the extralarge memories of one more Christmas I want to forget, Katherine walks in.

"What are you doing?" she asks me, but stares at the trash can.

"Just sorting dirty laundry."

"Didn't your mom just wash them?"

"Yeah, but they'll never come clean."

Katherine shakes her head. Knows I'm not going to explain, so she changes the subject. "You going home for Christmas?"

"I think I'll stay here and see what kind of tree they get."

Christmas Carol

"Marty, phone's for you. It's some man," Elizabeth yells down the hall from the lounge.

I am really tired now. First Jackie, then Mom and the sprints down memory lane. "Take a message."

"I can't, my nails are drying."

"You picked up the phone, didn't you?"

"I thought it was for me!"

"JEEEESSSuuuuusssssssss!"

"Stop swearing, Marty, and go pick up your call," Nurse Brown yells from her station.

"I wasn't swearing, I was singing. You didn't let me finish the song."

"Well, finish it on your way to the lounge."

I walk past Nurse Brown and sing, "JEEEESSS-uuuuusssssssss was booornnn. . . ." In the lounge I grab the phone and have one last yell at Her Highness Queen Elizabeth, "Pack up your princess pink polish and piss off."

She sticks her Tudor tongue out at me and leaves.

"Hello . . . HELLO . . ." Nobody is there.

Brrrinng.

"Yes."

"Marty?"

"Dad?"

"Yes! It's not some man – it's your father, and what the hell is going on there?"

"Nothing."

"As usual. Look, Marty, I'm calling to let you know I'm not sure I'll be able to bring you to Canada to see your grandmother for Christmas."

First call in the sequence. Second call will be the I-probably-won't-be-able-to. Third and final call being the I-definitely-can't. I'll save you some quarters, Dad. "It's okay. I'm Christmased out already."

"I thought I heard someone singing carols when I called the first time."

"We were practicing for the Christmas Pageant. We've got lots of Jesuses but only one Mary, right next door in the psych unit."

"Have they decorated your unit?"

"Yeah. They went all out," I say, and look beside me at the plastic poinsettia stem that's been collecting dust since someone stuck it in the cactus plant years ago. "We, ah, have Christmas plants and flashing red lights." I wave to the camera in the corner.

"Well, it sounds like you're all set. I'll talk to you next week and I should know more by then."

"Thanks for calling, Dad."

"You're welcome. And good luck with your play."

DAY 194
DECEMBER 24

Sleigh Ride

Mom and I walk past all the other cars in the parking lot to get to hers. The sun melts my goose bumps. Heat from the baked asphalt rises through my shoes and warms my feet.

I turn to see if anyone is watching. Lily's nose and palms are pushed up against a window. Mesh wire in the glass makes her look like a puppy being left behind at the pound. She turns her head away just as I mouth the words *see you soon*. A hand lands on Lily's shoulder and pulls her from the window.

"Watch out!" Mom yells.

My knee collides with her car.

"Are you okay?" she says, looking at the bumper.

"I didn't do it on purpose."

"I . . . I know. You just have to be more careful." Mom digs through her purse, comes up with the remote, beeps off the alarm, and unlocks the doors. I get in my side and help to remove the cardboard protector that keeps the dash from prematurely aging. Mom folds it up like an accordion and puts it in the backseat. She gets in and takes the club off the steering wheel and places it behind my seat.

I try to sit like an egg in its carton.

"Maybe we should get your hair cut on the way home?" Mom suggests, as she snips with her fingers at my bangs. "Miguel and Carlos would love to see you."

"I'm not really up to seeing anyone." I push the button for the window and stick my head out.

Mom starts the car and backs up with the parking break on. She figures that out at the stop sign to exit the lot. "Damn it!" She turns to me. "What about some new clothes?" She tugs on the thigh of my orange sweats.

I don't know if it's an invitation or a threat. I just want to go home and get in the ocean. I want to smell like salt instead of sausages. "No. Thanks."

Mom pulls a U-turn. The tires squeal for the first time in their lives. She guns it up the on-ramp and hits the freeway doing twenty miles over the speed limit.

"Do up that window! I just had my hair done."

And the nails.

"Use my cell and call Miguel. Tell him you don't want the appointment."

"What appointment?"

"The one for you at 3:00."

"Better slow down, Mom."

"Okay, how about I take my foot off the gas and you downshift that attitude of yours and tell me what your problem is?"

Here we go. "Which one do you want to hear about?"

"Don't get smart with me. I've gone to a lot trouble to make this a special Christmas and I'm not going to let you ruin it for anybody."

Anybody? "Is Gramma here?" I sit on my hands and cross my fingers.

"No, she's staying in Florida," Mom says, looking at the speedometer. She taps the brakes.

"Then, who?"

"It's a surprise. And part of the surprise was new hair and nice clothes. You'll want to look good." Mom steers the car across three lanes of traffic and just makes the off-ramp. "You got a problem with that?"

"No." I figure being a barbie is better than ending up a crash test dummy.

Surprise

Shopping is over. Home.

Mom parks the car away from the olive trees and where she'll be able to see it from her bedroom. She puts the club on the steering wheel and pops the trunk. I get out to retrieve the canvas car cover. I grab it and the bag with my not-nice clothes.

"Leave the bag. Get it later." I look around the trunk lid and Mom's face is talking to me from the side-view mirror. The sun reflects off her teeth.

I close the lid a little too hard as Mom gets out. She jumps and drops the keys. She dusts them off, fumbles with the remote, sets off the alarm, the flashers, and finally hits LOCK. She pats the car. "I know it's been a rough day."

We unfold the car cover like it's the national flag and drape it over. I kneel down on the pavement to put the steel cable that used to lock my bike under the belly of the car and through the brass rings in the canvas to lock it so no one can steal the cover.

Mom yanks on a corner to get out the wrinkles. "There you go. All tucked in."

I brush the dirt off my new brown pants.

Mom brushes them after I'm done. "Those size sixes look great on you. Now that you've put on some weight and I've lost some, we're about the same size. Maybe you'll let me borrow them. They're much better than those size ten jeans you wanted."

She starts to mess with my hair.

I take a deep breath . . . exhale slowly . . . while counting to ten.

"I just want you to look nice for your surprise."

Zack is here. She's probably wrapped him up and put him under the tree. I want to go back to the unit, crawl into bed, and sleep through Christmas.

Mom applies her lipstick from two different tubes because no one ever makes the right shade for her — something between Dusty Rose and Rose Mist. She flicks her mirror shut like Captain Kirk would his communicator. Linking her arm through mine, she leans on me while changing into the creamy higher heels she bought while we were shopping for me. I know she's spent money we don't have today.

160

"This is going to be the best holiday," Mom says, and heads toward the apartment. "Hurry up, Marty, before I melt in this parking lot."

At our door she hands me the keys. Her hands are shaking. Before I get the key in, the door opens from the inside.

"Hello."

"Dad . . ."

Mom pushes past me and stands beside him. "Merry Christmas, Marty. Do you like your surprise?"

I'm speechless. I thought I had no memories of the three of us together. But I do now. Pictures of them fighting. Yelling and throwing things. And doors slamming and always someone leaving.

Black-and-White Christmas

"Would you like a scotch?" Mom asks Dad, who is perched on the arm of the couch.

"Ah . . . sure. With a —"

"A lemon twist. I remember." Mom pulls a new bottle from the cereal cupboard. Opens the fridge for a lemon, the freezer for some ice. I have a good view from the barstool at the kitchen counter. *Beer. Second shelf. Vodka. Underneath the frozen corn.*

Mom makes the drink and delivers it to him, swirling the ice before she hands it over. Sounds like rocks hitting glass.

I flinch.

"You okay, honey?" Dad asks me, as he accepts the scotch. "Thanks, Judith."

"Yeah, I just have a headache."

"Biting your fingers isn't going to make it go away." Dad looks disgusted at my ripped and bleeding cuticles.

Mom walks to her bedroom. "I'll get you some Tylenol."

"I know you're a little shocked, Marty. Your mother said you wanted me to come to San Diego for Christmas, and she thought it would be better as a surprise." He sips his drink.

"I never –"

Mom rushes back. Stands between Dad and me. Thrusts the pills and water at me.

I dry my lap with a tea towel. "I never thought you'd actually make it," I say.

"Well, I'm here, but I think I'll go back to my room, have a nap, and get into some fresh clothes. My hotel isn't far from where your mother has made reservations for dinner, so I'll just meet you guys there." He tosses back the last half of his scotch.

I remember something. He usually drinks a lot slower.

Hearing Loss

Dad has escaped. And left me here.

"Why did you lie?" I look at Mom, but she just keeps washing the scotch glass.

162

"I didn't," she says, smiling at the sink. "You said –"

"No. I said nothing."

"I wanted to make you happy."

"By making me spend time with two people who can't even have a civilized phone conversation?"

"We're not just two people. We're your parents!"

"I've never seen you together!" My voice rises to match hers.

Mom looks like she's going to cry. "Don't be mad . . . it's Christmas."

"When am I allowed to be mad?"

Mom narrows her eyes. "Don't blow it, Marty. You'll regret it for the rest of your life. Trust me on this one."

"Trust you? That's a good one, Mom." I slide off the stool, step into my room, and slam the door. And listen.

The cereal cupboard bangs shut.

Bon Appétit

Mom won't tell me where we are going for our Christmas Eve dinner. I walk downwind from her. I only smell Opium by Yves Saint Laurent. Not scotch by Johnny Walker.

After two blocks I see Dad standing out front of *Mi Casa Su Casa*. I used to come here a lot with Cherri and her family for rolled tacos and hugs from Hernando.

"Hello, ladies." Dad gives me a kiss on the cheek. Hesitates. Gives Mom one too.

They both laugh.

Don't throw up before dinner . . . maybe after.

Dad lets Mom go in first. She heads for the hostess.

I can't move. He puts his hand on my back and pushes me into the restaurant. "What's the name of this place in English?"

I tell him, "My house is your house."

"The owner must have gone through a divorce." Dad laughs, "Don't tell your mother I said that."

Hernando busts through the saloon doors of the kitchen. "*Hola chica!*" He comes barreling towards us and wraps me up in one of his hugs. It's like being inside a warm soft tortilla. He used to do it to Cherri and say, "Look, we are a *pescadito* taco." He lets me go, but grabs my face and squeezes till I have fish lips. "*Tu cara es redonda! Está preciosa!*"

"What did he say?" Dad asks.

"That my face is fat." I look at Hernando. "*Mi padre no habla español.*"

Hernando shakes Dad's whole arm. "Oh, sorry, señor. Not fat. I'm fat. I say her face is round, beautiful!"

Dad smiles. "Looks like your mother is waiting for us."

"Yes. *Bueno!* Come, sit." Hernando leads us to Mom and a table near the kitchen. He surprises her by giving her a squeeze. "I be right back," he says.

Dad and I sit.

"This is not the table I requested," Mom says, standing and looking around.

"It's perfect, Judith," Dad says. He gets up and pulls out her chair.

The waitress brings chips and salsa. "Can I get you some drinks?" She smiles, but stops when she gets to me. "Marty?"

"Hi, Lucinda." We were in the same class last year.

"I'm sorry, I didn't recognize you. . . . You look good."

"How about a pitcher of virgin margaritas?" Dad suggests.

"Sure." Lucinda leaves, but talks to the hostess before going to the bar.

Dad puts his menu on the extra chair. "What's good here, Marty?"

"Everything. The *taquitos* are the best." *Don't screw up.*

Mom opens her menu and starts making faces. "I think I'll have the broiled chicken with salad instead of rice and beans."

Lucinda drops off the drinks and takes our order.

"You two must come here a lot," Dad says, and offers me some chips.

I take some. They are hot and greasy and the best-tasting thing I've eaten in months.

"I've never been here, but obviously Marty has. I'm working seven days a week. Doesn't give me a lot of time for going out," Mom says.

"Don't you and Marty eat together?"

"I'm going to the bathroom." I get up quickly and walk through the door. I look in the mirror to see the girl that everyone but my parents see. I go back to find out if reappearing makes any difference.

Hernando is delivering our food: "Here you go, two *taquitos especiales* and one grilled *pollo*. Enjoy. *Feliz Navidad*."

"Merry Christmas." Dad raises his glass and we clink. "Now how do you eat these things that look like cigars?"

"Señor, just like you'd smoke them – with your mouth and fingers." Hernando walks away laughing.

Dad and I eat with our hands. Mom picks at her salad. Mine is the cleanest plate they take away. No one wants dessert.

"Well, what should we do now, Judith?"

"It's a beautiful night. We could walk to the Grande Hotel and go dancing?"

"I can't go in there, Mom, I'm under age."

"I hadn't thought of that."

Yeah, right.

Silence.

"Actually, why don't you two go? It's been a long day. I haven't been in my own bed for almost six months. I could use a good sleep." I kiss Dad and leave before they know what hit them. I run across the street to the corner with the big hedge. Stop and catch my breath. Notice that all the palm trees are wrapped in Christmas lights.

I watch them come out of Hernando's and walk north to the hotel.

The lights are blurred all the way home.

DAY 195
DECEMBER 25

Alfresco

I hear Mom tiptoe through my room into my bathroom. She fluffs the new pink towels that will show stains and that have replaced my black ones. The toilet lid squeaks when she lifts it, checking for evidence. I cleaned it last night after I threw up and before I took a tranquilizer with a NyQuil chaser.

Mom sits on my bed. "Wake up, pumpkin. Come see what's in your stocking."

Play dead. Maybe she'll go away.

"Come on, I know you're faking. Your father will be here in an hour. I need you to make your famous eggs Benedict." She gets up and goes to the living room, expecting me to follow.

As I come out of my room, "White Christmas" by a reggae band blasts me in the face. Mom starts dancing around. She motions me to join her. I go straight to the kitchen and rip open the bag of oranges next to the juicer.

Mom shimmies over and lowers the volume. "Hope you don't mind I moved your stereo. It sounds so much better out here." She cranks it back up and starts to merengue.

I melt half a pound of butter for the hollandaise sauce. Burn it. Start over. The two eggs I try to crack one-handed end up crushed. Deep breath. I get a knife, tap three eggs gently, separate the yolks and whisk them into a heavy saucepan. Squeeze the life out of one fat lemon and stir that in too. Salt. Pepper. I cut six thick slices of honey ham and lay them in a hot cast-iron fry pan. They sizzle and *pop* and make my stomach snarl and chew on itself. It's starving from having to give up last night's dinner. And it's used to being fed twice by now.

Pounding at the door makes me jump. I go round the corner and peek through the spy hole. It's Dad.

"Jesus Christ, Marty! I've been knocking for five minutes. If you wouldn't play your music so loud, you might've heard me." Dad drops his gift bags and throws his sunglasses on the table.

I run to turn down the stereo.

Mom charges out of her bedroom in her bra and unzipped jeans. Her face and throat are slathered with green slime. "Hey, I was listening to that while I'm getting ready!"

"Dad's here." I point to the kitchen behind her.

"Merry Christmas, Judith."

Mom holds up the *one-minute* finger as she backs into her room.

"Sorry I yelled at you," Dad says, kissing me on the cheek. "That smells mouthwatering."

My mouth agrees.

"Can I help?" He drums his fingers on the counter.

"Sure. The English muffins need toasting. Cutting board and toaster under there." I put the ham in the oven. Whisk butter into the sauce. Add more lemon juice into boiling water, and eggs for poaching.

"When did you learn to be such a good cook?"

"Don't know." *When Mom was too busy working and drinking.*

"I read that anorexics like to cook – in a book I bought." He stares into the toaster.

"Was it a recipe book?" I try to joke.

Mom emerges zipped and decreamed. "Breakfast looks under control. I've already set the table." She opens the glass doors to the balcony. Everything out there is new to me. Table, chairs, cutlery, dishes, even cloth napkins.

Our old dishes are plain white. I picked them. A blank canvas to show off my artwork. I pull out the three I've had warming in the oven. Mom hands me yellow plates with blue flowers all over them instead. I put six million calories onto them and hand them back.

"This is delicious. Must be nice to be able to eat outside all year round," Dad says.

This is the third meal in two years I've choked down out here.

Presenting

Mom gets a silk scarf and perfume from Dad. Tiny gold earrings from me, bought during a Silver Lake field trip.

Dad gets a golf shirt from Mom. History of America's Cup yacht race from me.

I get a yellow sweater from Mom. Perfume and silver earrings from Dad. My stocking has chocolates. New underwear, three sizes bigger than last year.

169

Dad puts his stuff in one of the gift bags he brought. "I thought maybe we could take a ride. I want to look at some commercial property in La Jolla and Del Mar."

"That sounds great . . . ," Mom says, dabbing on her perfume.

"What time should Marty and I be back for dinner?" Mom freezes. "5:00."

"Okay, kid. Throw on some clothes, bring a jacket, and come see what Santa loaned me."

I move faster than a flying reindeer.

"You guys have fun. I'll do all the grunt work." Mom bangs the door shut after us.

We walk down the two flights to the lot. The car is parked right next to the building in a tight spot. I can't even get my door open.

"Just hop in," Dad says.

I jump in the red Mustang convertible and look up to the balcony. Mom is standing there. She looks like she got a pony for Christmas, but it got away.

Dinner

Dad and I are an hour late getting back. Everything has dried up, waiting for us. Including any Christmas spirit.

The frozen pumpkin pie burnt in the oven. Dad leaves before finishing his coffee.

"Throw it all out," Mom says, as she marches to her room, "including the tablecloth you spilt red wine on."

"I'm sorry. I can get it out."
"You can't fix what's already ruined."

DAY 196
DECEMBER 26

Boxing Day

I stumble to the kitchen, hung over from doubling my own prescription for sleep. Note on the coffeemaker.

> Your father called last night. He wants you to meet him by the hotel pool for lunch and a swim. Since the two of you have plans, I've gone to work.

I walk along the breakwater of the bay. Jump from boulder to boulder, my bare feet soft from months of being in slippers. I don't feel the cuts till I walk across the lawn of Dad's hotel to the pool.

I look for Dad through a hole in the privacy hedge.

His position is twelve o'clock. He is flanked by a blonde at eleven, a piña colada at one, and a brunette at two. I don't feel comfortable at three.

I swim home to drown myself in the deep end of a vodka bottle.

No Real Damage

Note on my bathroom mirror.

I couldn't wake you. Hope you had a nice sleep. I didn't even realize you were home last night till your father called at ten screaming at me because you never showed up yesterday. He says he called you all afternoon and then came over, but you weren't home. He thinks you blew him off for Zack. I warned you about blowing this. He's really pissed, Marty. He'll be over at 9:00 A.M. to talk to you. Don't leave. I've gone to work. Somebody has to.

Time: 8:30 A.M. I brush my teeth. Gently. My head aches so bad my hair hurts.

Knocking on the door.

"Marty, it's me. I watched your mom leave. I know you're there!" Zack yells.

Not good. I open the door. "You have to go now!"

His eyes grow big, so they can take in all of the new me. "I wanted to see you."

"Well, you have. My dad is in town and you don't want to see him."

"For once in her life she's right," Dad says, coming out of the stairwell. "Leave and don't come back."

"Please," I whisper to Zack.

Zack turns on Dad and says, "You're a jerk. I've been here for three years. Where've you been? Not here, picking her up when she faints. Or trying to get her to eat or not puke."

"I also didn't call you asking advice on how to control my daughter. You remember phoning me about that?" Dad fires back.

Zack retreats and says, "One day, Marty, maybe you'll make your own decisions. I'll be gone by then." He leaves.

"Me too," Dad says, "because between your lack of effort and the way I've been used, I don't see a reason to stick around."

I start to cry.

"Tears never work with me," he says, heading for the stairs. "Just ask your mother."

He's really leaving. For good. I run to Mom's bedroom window. Just like when I was little. I see him walk across the parking lot. *No. Don't go. Don't leave.*

Little kid. Powerless.

He's at the car. His bags are in the backseat. *He was leaving before he got here.*

My fist goes through the window. My anger flies away. Bravery bleeds out my knuckles.

Dad runs back.

I'm happy to see him. Scared.

He walks right over the broken glass I'm standing in. Takes my hand. Examines it. Picks out pieces of glass. "No real damage. I've had enough of your bullshit. I give up. Get a job. Go to school. Do something. A flight leaves for New York in two hours. I'll be on it. Tell your mother after I'm gone." He washes his hands in the kitchen. Slams the door when he leaves.

I go to my bathroom. Throw up. Take some Gravol.

Zack gone. Dad. Gone. Mom. She'll never forgive me. My fault. Cherri shouldn't talk to me. Lily. I didn't say good-bye.

"Silver Lake Institute. May I direct your call?"

"Eating disorder unit. Patient phone . . . please."

"ED unit, nurses' station," answers a voice I don't know.

"Ah, they made a mistake. I was trying to reach a patient."

"Your name and who you are calling, please?"

"It's Marty Black. I'm a patient. I want to talk to Lily."

"Marty, I'm very sorry. That's not possible . . . Lily passed away last night. Hang on, I'll get Rhonda."

I hang up.

Today is not real. Today needs to go away forever.

I look at the prescription bottle for a long time.

Tranquilizers. *Tranquil. Peace.*

ONE TABLET EVERY EIGHT HOURS AS NEEDED.

I take them all. And get into bed. And cry. And stop.

No more sad.

No more mad.

No more harm.

End of expectation, pressure, disappointment.

The last leaving.

DAY 204
JANUARY 3

The Psych Ward

Journal Entry # 3

I've had this place all wrong. The *loony bin*. It's not a bin. Nothing like it. A *bin* sounds like something you can climb out of. Push the lid off and scramble out. I've seen squirrels do it. Maybe that's where they hide their nuts too. But this place isn't a bin. This place is a pit. Not a pit with dirt sides. Dirt would be nice. There is no dirt in this hole with stainless steel walls and a white tiled floor. The glare from the hide-nothing lights reflects their shiny surfaces. Reflects everything back at you. You cringe and squint and squirm and try to squeeze your mind under the locked doors. There is nowhere to hide and yet I am invisible. Everyone here is invisible. *This is hell*. I thought I was in hell before, but now I know I was only hanging out in the lobby.

> Signed, M.

Journal Entry # 4

They are in their own little world here. No one paces with them. Fears with them. Cries with them. Only them. Only their world. I'm not in their world. But they are in mine. I have to live in both. Just one would be a luxury. A vacation from this both-worlds existence. The "real world" puts them here. Tries hard to remember to forget them. I want to yell, "Don't forget about me!"

It's so frightening I can't afford to be scared. I can see why they might shut down. You can't think about being in here too much. It would drive you crazy. So maybe that's why they invent other worlds. Escape the real one. Run from the one they can't handle to make one that they can.

It's the people on the staff that don't make sense. The "only thems" have it the right way round. One of them left their world today and entered mine. Made a big entrance. She walked over and put her face in my face. Looked into my windows to see if I was home. I stayed hidden, but she wouldn't go away. So I stared back at her. Startled her. That's when she drove her pencil about an inch into my shoulder. Wiped my skin off her dagger and onto her shirt. Then sat down to finish her crossword. It's not fair. The pencil got to be a pencil again. I'll never even get to be the person I didn't like before.

That's why I need to write this down. So I'll know exactly when I left for a vacation. 'Cause if I stay here much longer, I'm going to have to leave.

Signed, M.

Journal Entry # 5

The blackness is back. Returned early from its vacation. I guess it was jealous of the white enjoying itself so much. The white floor, white sheets, the white of the nurses' skin. Don't these people ever see the sun? I swear they hide in this cave during the day, drinking blood out of mugs, punch out in the basement, change into their little bat suits, then fly up the furnace chimney. I don't know how else they would get out. All the doors are locked. Including mine.

I get stabbed and they lock me in my room. I can see Crossword Kruger through my window, which takes up half of my door. The white window frame makes a border around the picture of the world outside. Like a Polaroid.

I make a shadow puppet of a snake. My albino python eats the Polaroid of the person who sits at her table and doesn't stab anyone else but me. All these crazy people to choose from. And I'm the one they put in isolation.

Signed, M.

Journal Entry # 6

There's too much time to think in here. My brain is bored with inventing the secret lives of the nursing staff. My fists have unclenched. Given up the fight. Tired of being constantly pissed off. I don't want to let go of the anger. 'Cause I know what happens. The sadness moves in and takes up more room than I can spare. It makes the water leave my eyes, it needs so much. The anger is a far more gracious guest. It takes up only a little bit of space. Doesn't need a lot to keep it happy.

The sadness took over my whole body when Lily died. I asked it to move nicely. It wouldn't. So I tried to kill it. And I thought I had. But I can hear it knocking. Standing on my porch with too many bags. Bags with names on them. Lily. Mom. Dad. My childhood. My future. My now. This is no overnight stay.

Signed, M.

Journal Entry # 7

I opened the door to the sadness last night. I had no choice. I cried all night. Shed water for the dead. Like in Frank Herbert's *Dune*. It is the most honorable act you can do for the dead. I am not honorable. I had no choice. They drank their coffee and stared while I shed water for Lily. For myself. It must have told the watchers something. Their smiles were gentle. Almost caressing. Why couldn't they have put Lily's heart on suicide watch? It killed itself and took Lily with it. Took me too. Or should have.

I can hear Lily's parents. I bet they were dry-eyed in their belief that God took her. God didn't take her. They sacrificed her to him. If there is a

God, he wouldn't take her. He would accept her. She was good. Innocent. But maybe he did take her. Out of mercy.

And if there is a God and if he is merciful, why didn't he take *me*? God even had a long time to think about. It took them a long time to realize I wasn't just sleeping. God had eight hours before they figured it out. I think he put some serious thought into it while I was "clinically" dead. Seventeen minutes. Probably the time it took for Lily to talk him out of handing me a pair of size-small wings. *Medical miracle.* That's what the doctor said. I think it was just a long conversation. Then a five-day coma. Perhaps more debate. Maybe Lily didn't want me. And God has left me here to punish me for letting her down. For letting everyone down. Including me. God is not merciful. He is right.

Signed, M.

Journal Entry # 8

Woke up for dinner. Actually, they woke me up. Tried to strangle my upper arm with the blood pressure cuff thing. They tried using the adult cuff, but they had to wrap it around so many times that it wouldn't work right. I told them to get a child's cuff. That's what they used on the other ward.

The other ward. That's what I used to call this ward. Used to call the patients in here *the others*.

Guess everything just depends on what side of the locked door you're on. The *theys* will always be the *theys*. Some things have to stay the same.

Signed, M.

Journal Entry # 9

I think the drugs have worn off. All the drugs. All the drugs I took and all the drugs they pumped into me to make them "untook." I'm feeling better. I think. At least I don't feel my face scrunching up like a piece of used paper. Maybe my face is recycling. Into what? Not a happy face – like ones you see on stickers and T-shirts. Those things force other people to smile when they look at them. My new face must be blank. 'Cause when anybody looks at me, all I get back is a blank. But blank is better than scrunch. I'm really roaring out of the starting gate, Dr. Katz – thanks for sticking me in here.

I do have Dr. Katz to thank for this journal though. There is nothing to do here without it. At least I'm moving. Or part of me is moving. My hand. Better than nothing. Because it would be so easy to not move. At all. Most of the time I feel like I could not move forever. Just stay still and safe. Blend into this place. Like a flake of dandruff in a snowbank.

But then I look at the cats (catatonics) out my door window. They remind me of those bronze statues you see in parks. The ones that sit on benches, or lean against lampposts. Out of the corner of your eye they look real, and then you realize they're fake.

This place is not a park. When I look out, I see the statue people sitting in chairs or leaning against the wall. I look straight at them and think they're fake. And then remember they are real. And that people are probably looking for them like they'd look for lost dandruff. I'm not sure I want to be found. Doesn't mean I don't want to be looked for.

So I guess I have to keep moving.

I've been staring at the "keep moving" sentence for five minutes. Or maybe an hour. Hard to tell. Funny though. As soon as I figure out that moving is what I have to do, I stop. I don't need a head-shrinker to point that out. Although I'm sure they would be excited to read that observation. And I'm not even afraid for them to read this stuff. I don't think they are trying to trick me. So I'm not a para-noid. And I don't want to be a catatonic. I'm fed up with being an anorexic. Ha-ha-ha.

So what am I supposed to be?

Signed, M.

DAY 216
JANUARY 15

Emergency

I wake up. I think that the crazy lady who stabbed her pencil into my shoulder has gotten into my room and jammed her pencil in my ear. I draw my hand slowly from under the sheets and run it up the side of my face and feel my ear. There is nothing in it. Not even a sound. I pull on it and it fills with pain.

Ear infection.

I've had them before. Lots of them. So many that a doctor decided to take my tonsils out to make the ear infections go away. It didn't work. The infections stayed. He should have cut out my ear instead of my tonsils. They didn't give me ice cream. I wouldn't have eaten it anyway. But right now, if they offered me a scoop, I'd take it and stick it in my ear. My ear is so hot, it wouldn't just melt the ice cream. It would vaporize it.

I sit up. Carefully. PAIN.

Open my eyes, just a little. Enough to see the dim lights outside my door and the bright desk light at the nurses' station. *Middle of the night.* I feel a yawn entering my nose, which is a weird place to start. But I can't open my mouth. At all. There must be a hundred rubber bands circling under my chin round the top of my head. My bottom jaw feels like it's going to swallow my face and bite my brain. The yawn, having come into my body, now wants to leave. But the doors are locked. My throat blows up like a bullfrog's. The yawn, now desperate, finds a side window to escape through and explodes out my ear. Shards of white glass fly behind my eyelids.

I want to black out, but searing aftershocks keep ripping through my ear and tearing down my neck. Tears squeeze out my eyes. I remember the surgeon saying that everything is connected. I remember the anesthesiologist saying to count backwards from one hundred. I need both of those guys right now. But I'd settle for a vet. If he couldn't fix my ear, he could at least put me to sleep.

I stand and walk like I've got books on my head. My door is locked. Of course. I knock on my own window to get someone's attention. The sound waves become nails hitting the hammer in my ear. Dizzy. Nauseous. The floor comes up to meet my tailbone. *Crack.*

I crawl away, in case a nurse heard me, rushes in, and slams me with the door. Back to bed. Like a sick old dog with my tail between my legs. Only I think my "tail" is now off to the left. My heart has moved into my ear and is pounding like a kettledrum. Everything is in the wrong place. Including me.

I finally make it to the bed. I try to pull myself up, but it's like I'm on a glacier. My fingers can't get a grip on the smooth white surface. I need an ice pick. Or at least finger-nails. I shouldn't have eaten them. I grab at the covers near the end of the bed, but they just keep coming at me like a rope with no one at the other end. I slide back to the floor. Someone moans. I move my eyes to find them. *I'm alone.* The moaner is me. *Where the hell is somebody?*

I lie down on the floor. Unborn-baby style. But it's not a womb, warm and soft and human-smelling. It's cold and hard and bleachy. For once I'm glad they wash the floors so much. And empty the garbage.

'Cause I'm going to throw up. I grab the metal bucket.

Olympic events begin in my body. My tongue starts to swim in saliva. My stomach gets in the ready position. Crouches down like a sprinter in the starting blocks. Puke pole-vaults up my throat, but hits the bar of my teeth. Vomit squeezes through like toothpaste. The force of my choking pushes the rest through a lot faster.

I'm done. *Just kill me now.*

Black.

Blinding white.

Must be on the bullet train to heaven. I squint to see who my welcoming angel is. I hope it's Lily.

No luck.

"Marty! . . . Marty, can you hear me? Did you take something? What did you take?" the nurse yells at me.

I try to shake my head *no*, but I don't think it moves.

"You better tell me right now!" she says, as she snaps on rubber gloves. From my chin she swipes a fingerful of vomit and brings it to her nose. She inhales deeply.

I gag and point to my ear and moan.

"Your ear hurts?" she asks.

I moan again.

She grabs my face and cranks my head to the side. "It's all red." She puts her unrubberized wrist against my fore-head. "And you're hotter than Hades. Bloody hell, I thought you OD'd!" she says, all pissed off like she's upset I haven't. She leaves.

My head is still spinning from her steering it so hard to the left.

She's back already, coming at me with her flashlight and a wooden shish kebab stick with a ball of cotton skewered on the end.

"On't sick at in eye ear," I plead.

"I can't understand you if you mumble," she replies.

I can't talk right with my jaw all screwed up, so I try telepathy. *Don't stick that in my ear! Don't! Don't! Don't . . . JESUS CHRIST!*

She turns the stick. Crust grinds and crackles, releasing hot lava.

"You sure are cooking something up in there," she says, as she looks at the stick with melted yellow goo on the end.

I must be roasting frigin' marshmallows.

"I better take your temperature."

Not up my ass you don't.

She searches her big nurse pockets. "I'll be right back," she says, and spins away, making her rubber Birkenstock clogs shriek, which makes me want to scream too. That and the air pressure she displaces upon her speedy return, weapon in hand. "I'm going to stick this in your other ear, okay?" she says, and holds out the thermometer thing that looks like a telephone receiver with a Pinocchio nose growing out of the earpiece.

I blink twice. Once for yes. And once as a thank-you to the God I don't believe in, but am grateful that he doesn't hate me as much as I hate him.

She gently slides the nose of the thermometer into my good ear. Apparently only bad ears are good for mashing things into. I exhale. Three seconds later, beeps are being fired into my ear, through my brain, and hit the bull's-eye of my bad ear. My eyes do backward somersaults in my head.

"102 degrees. No doctors around this time of night, and they'll just yell at me if I page them for an ear infection. You'll have to go to emergency. Let's get you off the floor and then I'll figure this out," she says, and lowers herself into a deep knee-squat, shoots her arms straight under my armpits like a forklift, and hoists me up onto the bed. She steps back and examines her lab coat. A puce-colored design in the shape of an inkblot test is what she sees. "Well, look at that mess."

I see a butterfly. I never see a butterfly in Katz's office. I wonder how many points I'd get now.

"Pull those clothes off while I get us both clean ones, and if you're going to throw up again, for God's sake, do it in the bucket." She daintily pinches her coat and holds it out from her chest as if she's pretending she has bigger boobs. She looks down and gains three chins. She leaves. Again.

I know she wants me to undress, but I can't seem to move. I'm so cold, the thought of being uncovered hurts worse than my ear. And she is going to be back in a nanosecond.

She returns, all white again. "Come on, Marty, you should have got that stuff off. You've got to help me. I'm short staffed tonight." She tears the sweatshirt over my head, yanks my sweatpants off, and leaves me sitting in my white socks, white underwear, and white spots in front of my eyes. I'm freezing. I want my down comforter from home. She throws a hospital gown at me. "Put that on."

I reach for my thin covers and start to lie down.

"Go back to sleep half naked if you want to, but no covers," she says, as she rips them from my hands. "You've got a fever and need to cool down. I need to find someone who can deal with this. I don't have the time."

Nurse Brown and I stand in the air lock – the space between the front doors of the building and the doors that open into the foyer. The security camera stares at me from its perch in the corner of the ceiling. The intercom on the wall says nothing.

She tries to open her umbrella. "Come on!" she says, and bangs it on the floor. She buzzes the reception desk. No answer. Security must be on a break. "Forget it." She throws the umbrella against the wall. She takes off her raincoat and holds it over my head. "You okay to walk fast to that yellow car in the second row?" She points to an old VW Bug that looks like it's being dented by the pelting rain.

I nod.

"Okay, here we go. You get the door."

We run-walk towards the car. I can't remember the last time I saw rain. I like rain. But not today. It comes down on my coat-roof like bombs. The sound explodes in my ear.

At the car, Nurse Brown nods at the passenger door and says, "Give it a yank." She holds the coat over my head until I'm all the way in, and then throws it into the backseat. She closes my door gently and runs around to the driver's side. She gets in.

She's soaked. Like she's just stepped out of the shower. She reaches into the pile of take-out coffee cups and fast-food wrappers at my feet and finds a paper napkin to dry her face.

All those times you ragged on me about my room . . . and you drive a pigsty.

"Sorry about the mess."

I forgot that she could read minds.

She opens her purse and roots around till she finds a pill bottle. Uncorks it and pours out a selection.

Great. I'm sick and she's taking meds.

She decides which one she wants, holds it in front of my face, and says, "It's Vicodin. If you can hold this down, it will make you feel better. Between you and me, I gave this to you at the institute. I'll put it in your chart when I get back. I could get in a lot of trouble, but you look like you're on the rack and you could be there awhile. Emerg might be backed up."

I stare at her. She isn't handing me a painkiller. She's giving me ammunition that I could use to shoot her down for good.

She pushes the pill between my teeth and bends over and fishes around my feet in the passenger's side till she pulls up a bottle of already-been-opened water. She holds it up and swishes it around and takes a good look for backwash asteroids. No sightings, I guess, because she unscrews the cap, hooks her baby finger into my cheek, pulls it out and pours a little water into it and a lot of water down my neck.

*Very unnursey. Very unhygienic. Very appreciated. I hope
she can read my mind on the last very.*

"You're welcome."

Of course.

The Waiting Room

Nurse Brown drops me off at the hospital entrance and
goes to find a parking spot. I go inside and tuck myself into
a corner of the waiting room. People start sneaking looks
at me. I look at myself. Tennis shoes – no laces, no socks.
Hospital gown hanging out from underneath a dripping
wet raincoat. I look like a mental patient who broke out of
the asylum. Not a mental patient with an ear infection,
busted out by Nurse Brown.

Nurse Brown runs in and scans the room. She spots
me. Question marks appear in her eyes and she makes the
okay sign with her hand. I give her the *okay* sign back
and she turns to find the triage nurse. I know that's what
she's doing. I'm a pro at emerg. Except for the last time, I
don't know what they did then. I was unconscious.

My teeth start chattering. I grab my face to stop
them. My cold hand feels good on my hot cheek. I put
my other hand / ice pack gently over my ear. I must look
like the hear-no-evil and speak-no-evil monkeys com-
bined into one.

The painkiller isn't doing much. *Maybe it was a
placebo.* I need the real thing.

I want my mom . . . mommy . . . mother. Why doesn't one of those words fit?

I want Her.

I don't feel like Her knows me. But she would know where to rub my head. If she could remember way back when. When I was just a little kid and she wasn't just my mom. She was my superhero. Until I was about ten years old and figured out that Wonder Woman wasn't supposed to drink silver bullets – she was meant to deflect them.

She's not here. Take care of yourself, Marty.

That phrase is so familiar. Maybe it has to do with what Dad said when I was small. He said, "Nobody is going to take care of you, but you." I don't remember the place or situation, but I remember the words – I always remember the words. Maybe they were the words said to him when his father died. And he remembered.

I look around the waiting room to see the other people who are supposed to take care of themselves. There is a yellow guy who looks like he used a cheap fake tanning cream. I don't think that's his problem. His eyes are yellow too. *Jaundice.* His friend tries to look relaxed while he reads a fashion magazine. A mother nuzzles a too-quiet baby. The dad has his arm around both of them and his eyes glued to the doors where the nurses come through to call who is next. An old couple sit holding hands. With his free hand, the man holds an oxygen mask to his face. Her free hand clutches her chest. They need a double room.

Nurse Brown walks towards me with a set of scrubs and a flannel blanket under her arm. She takes my hand. "I'm going to get you out of those wet clothes." She pulls me up slowly and doesn't let go. She puts her other arm around my waist. We do a my-back-to-her-front tango across the waiting room floor.

I'm feeling a little better. The Vicodin must be kicking in.

"There's more room in here . . . and it's cleaner than the bathroom," Nurse Brown says, as she opens the door to the linen supply closet. She leans me against a rack and closes the door. "I called your mother," she says, as she takes off my coat and robe, and unties my gown.

"And . . . ?"

She pulls a scrub top over my head and looks me in the eyes. "She said she would like to come, but she didn't think you wanted her."

We never think the same way. We think too much.

"So I called another nurse in to cover for me," Nurse Brown says, and gets down on one knee and puts my hands on her shoulders. She rolls up the pants for me to step into. My feet don't want to lift off the ground. I feel so heavy. She takes off my wet shoes and puts my feet in the pants for me. She pulls up the pants and wraps the blanket around me.

"I used to think you were a real bitch," I say.

"Well, Marty, I guess I could say the same about you," she says.

"Say what?"

"That I thought you were a bitch."

"I knew you could read minds!"

"Marty, you said the bitch thing out loud," she says, laughing.

"Oh, my God."

"That was out loud too. Don't sweat it. The Vicodin can make you a little loopy. It acts like a truth serum on some people."

"Is that why you gave it to me?"

"No. But it's going to be a nice bonus. I want to ask you some questions. And medicated or not, you have to be honest with me from this moment on if you want to get out of the psych ward and come back to the unit." Nurse Brown pulls socks out of her back pocket and kneels down to put them on my feet. She stays there. Just staring at the floor. She takes a deep breath and says, "Do you want to come back?"

"Yes."

"Are you going to eat?"

"Yes."

"Are you going to be a pain in the ass?"

"Probably."

Nurse Brown looks up at me half smiling, half wincing.

"You said I have to be honest."

"The last question was a test – you passed."

Sunfire

The doctor in emergency had given me a prescription of antibiotics and a standing order for Vicodin.

Nurse Brown drives us back to the institute and parks facing east. I start to get out of the car and she puts her hand on my shoulder and says, "Wait a minute, Marty. I want you to see something. Just look forward."

"To what?"

"To lots of these."

I don't have a clue to what she is talking about, but I stare straight ahead.

And then it happens.

I wonder if I'm hallucinating because it looks like the engine is on fire. The fire is not new. It is billions of years old. Sunfire.

The sunrise. It gets brighter. Blinding. As it climbs higher over the hood of the car and becomes framed like a crystal postcard by the windshield.

"When I work day shifts, I come early so I can do this. Just sit and watch the sun come up. It helps to keep me sane."

"I haven't seen a sunrise for a long time. Maybe that's why I'm crazy."

"You're not crazy, Marty."

"What do you call someone who tries to kill themself?"

"Full of pain."

"I'm not feeling any right now." I laugh.

"That's because of the painkiller. You have an ear infection and some physical pain, so I gave you *one* painkiller. You used to be violent, so the psychiatrist prescribed tranquilizers. But even he didn't know how much mental pain you were in. You tried to kill it with thirty times the normal dose. I don't believe you were trying to kill *you*, Marty, just the pain. Unfortunately, the *you* and the *pain* are tied to each other. You're not crazy."

I don't know what to say. So I say the first thing that pops into my head: "I killed Lily." I look at Nurse Brown. For a reaction to my confession.

Nurse Brown continues to stare straight ahead. Doesn't move anything but her lips. "How do you think you did that?"

"Lily was in my bed when she died, right?"

"Yes. She was lonely and upset. She missed you when you went home for Christmas, so she moved into your room."

"But my bed, right?"

"What's so deadly about your bed?"

"Remember when you made me scrape the toilet paper from my intercom?"

"That was months ago."

"I destroyed the wiring. . . ."

Nurse Brown turns and looks at me, cocking her head to one side.

"When Lily tried to call for help, it wouldn't work. If it weren't for me, you could have saved her."

Nurse Brown grabs my chin, turns my face to hers. She wipes my tears with her hand and leans across to put my head on her shoulder. She whispers into my ear, "Is that what you've been thinking?"

I nod. She rocks us gently.

"Her heart was damaged. And she'd starved it, and . . . oh, honey, Lily didn't have time to push a button."

After a while I open my eyes and look out the windshield. "The sun is gone."

"It's still out there. You just have to look for it."

Back in the Box

Nurse Brown asks, "Where do you want to go, Marty?"

"Back to my old room."

We walk through the institute in silence. It's peaceful. Too early for anyone to be up and going crazy.

So here I am. Staring at my old place by the window. "Is that my bed?"

"No. It's new. They took the old bed away because it freaked out the girls to have a deathbed on the unit."

Lily dying in this room must have been too much for Katherine and Catwoman because they are gone too.

Nurse Brown says, "Rest today, sleep tonight, because tomorrow you start."

"You mean start again."

"No," she says, "just start. Start fresh and keep it simple. You have to explain to the other girls why you tried to kill yourself. You really blew them away. You were the strong one. The one with the big mouth who didn't care about anything. Now you have to tell them the truth."

"I don't know what that is."

Nurse Brown smiles. "The doctor said the antibiotics should kick in, in about twenty-four hours. I'll give you thirty to find the truth. If your ear still hurts and you haven't found anything by 2:00 P.M. tomorrow, I'll give you another Vicodin. That should help solve your problems," she laughs.

"I've got a lot more than two problems. How many do you want to solve?"

"Not me. You. And you're going to do it one at a time."

Journal Entry # 10

I am alone. But not quite alone. Nurse Brown rescued my journal from the psych ward. We are grateful for her heroics. She also released a box of pens. Maybe she peeked (she wouldn't have had time to read much) and saw how much I'd written. Or maybe she knows. Just knows. Brought me all this ink so I wouldn't run dry.

Anyways, she tucked us all in before going home to get some sleep herself. She'll be back for 2:00 P.M. tomorrow (group therapy) when we return to our regular program of the crazy antics of anorexics and the nurse who breaks all the rules to save them.

I'm going to sleep now.

I wonder if Lily will visit me.

Signed, M.

Middle of the Night

I wake up not sure of where I am. Big room. Two empty beds. Door wide-open.

I'm not locked up. Not in the psych ward. I'm back in the unit. And I have a window. I look outside. The blue-black of the middle of the night stands silent.

I have to pee. Someone has left the bathroom light on for me. And someone has put a pair of those silly hospital slippers, which can also be used for shower caps, beside my bed. And someone is standing in my doorway.

"Nice to have you back, Marty," says Dennis.

"Did you miss me?"

"Like a third nostril."

"That much?"

"Maybe more."

"Admit it, it was boring without me."

"It was . . . quiet. Too quiet."

"Did you leave the fashionable footwear and the light on?"

"These floors are pretty cold and I thought you might get scared if you woke up in the dark by yourself."

"I don't get . . . thank you, Dennis."

"You're welcome. I have to check on the other girls. I'll be back with your meds."

My back stiffens. "What are they putting me on now?"

197

"Nothing new, just the antibiotics and a painkiller, if you need one."

I feel my ear. It's a little sore. Nothing like it was. I want a painkiller, but I don't need it. "Just the germ killers, please."

Dennis's black silhouette turns sideways and the light from the hall hits his face. I see his smile and then he is gone.

I snap the slippers on and head to the bathroom. It's so white when I open the door that it blinds me. I close my eyes and then the door. And switch off the light. I feel my way around in the dark, picturing the room I know so well on the insides of my eyelids.

I sit on the freezing toilet and immediately get goose bumps that raise me four inches off the seat. I wait but nothing happens. Finally my bladder thaws.

I could pee on myself to warm me up, but they'd throw me back in the loony bin. And I'm never going back there. Never.

"Never!" I say out loud, just to make sure I heard myself.

"Marty! You okay?" Dennis yells from the other side of the door.

I jump and pee myself. *Never say never.*

"Jesus Christ, Dennis, are you trying to scare me?"

"Sorry, I was bringing your meds and I heard you yell and no light from under the door and I got –"

"I'll leave the light on in the bathroom, so you won't get scared."

"Thanks, Marty."

"No problem. You did it for me. I'll be out in a couple of minutes. I want to take a quick shower."

"This time of night?"

"Yes. I need to . . . you don't want to know."

"Do you need anything else?"

I look around bathroom. There is nothing in it but me and the plumbing. "Actually, I need everything. Including something clean to wear."

"Towels, soap, and shampoo coming up. And a pile of clothes dropped off by your mom."

"My mom was here?"

"Let me get the stuff and we'll talk when you get out."

Feels good to smell of soap and spring-fresh dryer sheets.

Dennis comes in carrying a cafeteria tray of tea and shortbread cookies.

"I thought I couldn't have tea because of the caffeine? Is it herbal?"

"Nope. It's full octane. But I don't like to drink alone," Dennis says, as he hands me a big mug.

I take a sip. Bite off half a cookie. It melts into the best thing I've ever tasted. I shove in the other half. "What time was my mom here?" I say, and spray cookie all over Dennis. "Oh . . . I'm sorry."

"It's okay," Dennis laughs, brushing himself off. "Your mom was here around 11:00 P.M."

"I know it was after visiting hours, but you guys should've let her see me."

Dennis is silent.

"She didn't want to see me?"

"She didn't want to disturb you."

"I'm already disturbed."

"She's really afraid she'll upset you."

"She probably feels guilty for sticking me in solitary in the psych ward."

"Marty, it's mandatory for an attempted suicide to spend thirty days in the psych ward. And you only had twelve days under your belt . . ."

"They don't allow belts in there. Just pencils."

". . . And your mom had them put you in solitary after the other patient stabbed you. To protect you, not punish you. Your mom was here all yesterday afternoon meeting with Nurse Brown, the treatment team, and the board to get them to agree to let you back in this unit. Nurse Brown brought you back here, but it wasn't guaranteed that you could stay. Nurse Brown and your mom fought really hard because they both knew you'd go crazy in there."

"They were right. I owe them big time."

Dennis nods.

"She was here twice?"

"Yep."

"Doing things for me?"

"Everything she could."

"Except see me . . . and no one else has come to visit either."

"Nope. The other girls were afraid you'd tell them to fuck off."

"Have I really been that much of an asshole?"

Dennis doesn't answer. He just shoves a cookie in his mouth and chews and stares at me.

"I have to say sorry to a lot of people." The words squeak through a small hole in the back of my throat.

"It sounds selfish, Marty, but you have to forgive yourself first, before those apologies can mean anything."

"Is that part of the program for Alcoholics Anonymous or Anorexic Assholes?"

"Both."

Puts Mom and me in the same boat. "My mom told me not to tell my father about trying to ax myself. I think she's trying to protect herself."

"And you've never done anything to protect your interests – especially when you're scared?"

"I've done a lot of things – all of them bad."

"I doubt it, but your mom has done good things for you in the last twenty-four hours. Hang on to that. Try not to judge. Relationships don't work if you dictate how or what someone gives to you. You just have to accept what they can give," Dennis says, as he grabs a cookie, gets up, and walks into my bathroom. He comes back and hands me a fistful of toilet paper to dry my tears.

I take the paper.

"How about a cookie?" he says, crumbs spraying from his mouth.

I take the cookie. And stick my tongue out at him. It's hard to be gracious when you're blowing your nose into bum-roll.

Journal Entry # 11

They let me sleep till 12:30 P.M. The sun was shining on my bed through the magnifying glass of my window, keeping me warm.

They delivered my lunch at 1:00 P.M. I ate the same lasagna that was fed to me in the psych ward. It's a lie that this unit has its own special kitchen to suit our dietary needs. I won't tell the other girls. They'll go nuts.

1:30 P.M.

I have to face those other girls in half an hour. Thirty minutes to show time. But I think I found the material I need hours ago.

After Dennis left last night, I couldn't sleep (probably the tea), so I stayed up and read all the stuff I'd written in this journal. It's all over the place. Like someone who is lost and keeps making turns, then backtracking. Someone who is afraid to ask for directions. But I found what I was looking for. It was so obvious by its absence. And I'm not writing it down because then I won't be brave enough to tell the truth to anyone else.

1:54 P.M.

Signed, Marty

2:00 P.M. — Show Time

Nurse Brown comes to my room to personally escort me to group. I understand.

"Ready?"

"Yes."

"Good," she says, putting her arm around my shoulder

and steering me out into the hall. Ten paces and we arrive at the library / group therapy room.

Everyone is already here. Came early to get a good seat.

They flash me neutral, nervous smiles. Except Elizabeth. Hers is almost pleasant. And she doesn't look away.

There's a new girl. She doesn't look up at all. Just stares at the floor. I know what she's doing. *Been there. Done that.* Well, she's going to get her parents' money's worth today.

One chair left. Beside Rhonda. I walk through the middle of the circle and sit.

Rhonda puts her hand on mine. Gives me the *all-systems-go?* look.

I nod.

Rhonda clears her throat and says, "Okay, Marty, you can start."

My heart is pounding. *Start.*

My hands are shaking. *Start.*

My stomach is gargling bile. *Start.*

My throat is closing like elevator doors and the words are going to be trapped.

LEAP!

"Christmas at home didn't go so hot."

I hear lots of breath escaping. Including my own.

"It sucked. You probably guessed that because I swallowed $200.00 worth of this-will-make-you-feel-better." I laugh. Alone. "Truth is, I've been killing myself for a long time. But dying slowly just wasn't fast enough anymore. So I downed the bottle of happy pills so I wouldn't have to be sad anymore. So no one could be mad at me. So no one could ever leave me again. So I wouldn't do any more harm."

I look around. Katherine is crying. So are a couple of others. The new girl is stone-faced.

"Thank you, Marty," Rhonda says, and squeezes my hand. "Anybody have anything to add?"

Rhonda's not surprised. "Okay, take some time to digest what Marty has shared and we'll talk about it in group tomorrow. You have an hour and a half of free time before snack."

Everyone gets up to leave. Except me. And Rhonda. I don't know what I was expecting. *Loud wailing? High fives? A group hug?*

"Tough crowd," I say to Rhonda, after everyone is gone.

"I know what you mean, kiddo. I've been working this room for four years."

I turn to look at her. Her eyes are red. "You were crying."

"For joy, Marty. For joy."

"Why does Elizabeth seem strange?"

"She's been having shock therapy for depression."

"Holy shit."

"You were next on the list."

Back in my room. Now that I'm free to walk around, I can't think of a place to go.

Shock therapy. Shit. Almost. This close. Just thinking about getting shock therapy is shock therapy. I'm feeling better already.

Someone knocks on my door.

"Come in."

Katherine pushes the door open, but doesn't come in. "Did you mean it? About being lonely?"

"Did you come here to tell me you thought I was lying?"

"No," she says, as she pulls at something she'd left in the hall. She walks into the room, dragging her suitcase. Katherine throws her bag and her body onto her old bed. "I *thought* you might like some company . . . Mrs. Burns will be along in a minute."

DAY 222
JANUARY 21

Funeral Expenses

"Marty, telephone," calls a voice from the hall.

Must be Mom. Finally. Just be grateful. Try not to judge. I pick up the phone.

"Hi, Mom."

"No. It's your father."

I hold my breath. "Sorry . . . hi . . . Dad."

"Marty."

"Yes."

"If you ever pull another stunt like that again . . ."

"What stunt?"

"There have been so many, it's ridiculous. But the last one is the one I'm talking about."

The window . . . please let it be the window.

"If you ever try to kill yourself again . . . I'll pay for your funeral – but I'm not coming to it."

Mom told him.

"Did you hear me, Marty?"

Loud and clear.

"DID YOU HEAR ME?"

"Yes, Sir." I stand up straight.

"I'm not a sir! I'm your father."

Yes, Sir.

"Do you want a funeral or a father?"

Right now I'd like to be dead.

"It's up to you, Marty. I'm easy."

"No, you're not." *Oops.*

"You're right. I'm not. And, unfortunately, we're a lot alike. Because we are father and daughter. And it would be a lot easier if we started acting like it. Instead of hostage and keeper."

"Who is who?" *I've got nothin' left to lose.*

"I suppose right now it's hard to tell because I'm making all the demands. You can't keep hurting yourself to make me come running."

Never worked anyways.

"I am glad you're okay. Your mom said it was close."

I can hear Dad start to choke up.

"I know, Dad. Believe it or not, I am too." I can barely get the words out.

"After you get out, come to New York and visit. It's too late to be Daddy's little girl, but we can try the father and daughter thing. Maybe even live here for a while."

"Maybe."

"We could do lunch – I owe you one."

"Speaking of lunch . . ." *I have to get off the phone or I'm going to cry.*

"I know. You have to go . . . I do too. I'll call you tomorrow."

"You don't have to."

"I want to. I love you, Marty."

"I love you too, Dad."

Phone ~~Home~~

The phone rings nine times before the machine picks up. It's my voice on the message. It's weird to hear your own voice talking to you. My voice sounds so lifeless.

She kept the message all these months. I would have known that if I had phoned the house.

A million beeps. Then dead air.

"Hi, ahh . . . if you have time, maybe you could –"

"Marty?"

"Hi, Mom."

"I didn't recognize your voice."

"Are you screening the calls?"

"I don't feel like talking to anyone."

"You talked to Dad."

"I . . . called him."

"And told him what I had done after telling me not to."

"I know, Marty. Please, don't be mad. I was afraid he would blame me . . ."

I know all about that fear.

"And then I didn't know how to tell you I'd told him. I'm sure it was a shock."

"Thanks for saving me from the other kind."

"What was that?"

"Nothing, just thanks."

"What? Thanks for nothing?"

"Just the opposite."

"Okay . . . so how did it go with your father?"

"We're going to try something new."

"Marty, I know it hasn't always been that great, but I've tried to be a good mother and I know I have at times. If you give me another chance before you go live with him . . ."

"Apparently, I have to give myself a chance first. You should know that from AA."

"I do, Marty. I just didn't know you did."

"Why don't we try to start over when I get home?"

"That sounds good. We could have a starting-over party. For your birthday. You missed your birthday . . ."

I forgot all about my birthday. Or did I?

". . . You were in the coma, turning eighteen when you should have been out in the world. I sang 'Happy Birthday' to you. Did you hear me? Did you hear anything I said?"

"I'm sorry, Mom, I didn't. What day is it? It's hard to tell in here."

"It's one day at a time, Marty. One day at a time."

Uplifting

"Marty! Telephone. Again!"

I check the clock. *3:30. Must be Dad. Mom called already.*

"Hi."

"*Klein muisje?*"

"Mrs. Van Daal?" *I'm sure as hell not psychic.*

"Yes, leiveling. How are you doing?"

"I'm okay. You?"

"Bisy. Very bisy. I miss my little mouse."

"I'm not so little anymore."

"How much you weigh?"

"116 pounds."

"That is nothing. I weigh 100 pounds more. You need to catch up to me. I could bring you some food."

"No, you can't. They won't allow it."

"Why not?"

"They're afraid you might put something in it."

"Like what would I put in da food?"

"Taste."

"So you gain a sense of joke, too?"

"I regained it."

"Good! You going to need it when you come back to vork."

"Mrs. Van Daal, I . . . but –"

"No big buts, except mine," she laughs. "I already give you a raise. Your mother, she says you need uplifting."

"Thanks. I'll stop by when I get out."

"I buy you a coffee . . . and a donut."

DAY 239
FEBRUARY 7

Dolphins

"So you got a day pass," Katherine says, not bothering to hide her jealousy.

"Yeah," I say.

"Going anywhere special?"

"No. Just on the boat, with my ex-best friend."

"I didn't know you had a –"

"A boat? I don't. It's her family's."

"I was talking about the *her* – I didn't know you had a best friend."

"I did . . . once." *I had Cherri. Cherri Salmon was my best friend. Until I screwed that up too.*

So here I am on the boat. Sitting on the bow. In my old favorite place. A *before* place. And as long as I don't look back at the cockpit – at Willy steering, at Cherri's mom staring at me with worry, at Mr. Fish trying not to look at me, and Cherri, who is hiding down below – as long as I keep facing west, I can pretend that a lot of shit didn't happen.

It used to be so natural. Sitting here. It was my place. And everybody knew it. I belonged as much as the jib, the cleats, or the anchor. But it's different now.

I look over the side. At the water rushing by the hull. At my legs hanging over – two little white ropes, with ankles for knots and toes for frayed ends. The bow dips, and plunges my legs into the sea. And when the bow rises again, the water grips my bones like she wants to take me with her. But her fingers just slide across my skin. There is nothing for her to hang on to.

Out of nowhere come the dolphins to get a free ride in our bow wake. Beautiful isn't a big enough word to describe them. Steel blue. All rounded. No sharp edges. Fat. Fat and beautiful. And alive. I almost envy the figure-head, with her spine grafted to the bow. She's close enough to touch them, but her hands are tied behind her back. She can't plug her nose when her head gets dunked underwater. She has to hold her wooden breath. I realize I've been holding mine. It bursts out of me and makes a little whistle. The sound grabs the attention of a smaller dolphin. He rolls on his side and eyes me. Not asking, but daring me to join him. He looks naughty with his curly smile. He backpedals with his fluke to stay in the wake for more than his turn. A big dolphin nudges him and he sinks to move to the back of the line. *He'll be back.* The other dolphins don't pay too much attention to me. Too busy catching their waves. The spray from their blowholes kisses my mouth. I taste their wet salty breath. Here comes my guy again. Rolling over, working his fluke, head nodding, his weird triangle arms patting up and down, his whole body and his eye saying, "Come on in – the water's fine." His grin teases, "Chicken!" I can't stand it anymore – just watching. I reach out with my foot. To touch him. But the bow dips and I kick him in the belly. He dives and the playground monitor surfaces and snaps her bottled teeth at my toes and gives me *the look*. I've got detention. The rest go off to play somewhere else. I can chalk up another unique achievement. I'm the only person on the planet to ever piss off a dolphin.

My throat closes up and my face gets hot. The tears come uninvited. I watch them fall over the side. I'm wishing the dolphins would come back to taste my salty apologies. The way I tasted their breath. But they're really gone. My *I'm sorry's* always come too late.

"I'm tacking, barnacle!" Willy yells at me and spins the wheel like a Vegas roulette.

I grab hold of the lifelines and the boat heels over to my side. The jib makes a ripping sound as it comes across the bow and slams into my back, almost tearing me from the deck as it fills. It finally rests over the water, full of wind and satisfied.

I hear Willy cracking up, having pulled off one of his favorite tricks. He gave me the nickname "barnacle" 'cause I'm the only person who has never been dumped overboard by one of his terrorist tacks.

"Marty, are you alright?" Mrs. Fish calls, her voice too high.

"I'm fine," I say and turn to reassure her, but she sees the tears and thinks Willy made me cry. Mrs. Fish hauls off and whacks her twenty-year-old son across the back of the head like he's six. She says something to him. Too low for me to hear. And she smacks him again.

"I'm sorry, Marty!" he yells at me, and moves in case his mother isn't finished.

Now I know for sure things are bad. I know for three reasons. One: I've never seen Willy's mom hit him. And he has given her lots of opportunities. Two: Willy has called me everything except Marty. And three: he has never ever said "I'm sorry" to me for anything. Not the time I was taking a shower, when he picked the bathroom lock and poured a bucket of ice water on my head and I slipped on a chunk of ice and fell and sprained my wrist. Not that day that I had fallen asleep on the deck of the boat. He untied my top and waited till we were pulling into the yacht club to scream at me to get the mainsail down or we were going to crash, and I jumped up half asleep and didn't realize I had on only half a bathing suit till the gas dock boys started clapping. Willy ran to me laughing and said, "You better cover up those monkey bumps!" and handed me two Band-Aids. The worst was when he would pin me to the ground by sitting on my chest, with his knees on my shoulders. He would lean over till his face was about a foot and a half from mine. And smile. Then make fish lips and work up a wad of spit that he would let dangle from his lips a couple inches, and then he'd suck it back up into his mouth. Willy did this over and over, each time letting the elastic goober stretch an inch closer to my face. It was a game of chicken. Move or open your mouth to scream and he would lose his load and you'd being wearing it as face mask. Or worse. One time he did it to Cherri and she got her hand loose and grabbed his baggage. Cherri laughed and Willy dropped a lougie right into her mouth. She was so mad. She threw him off and ran into the house, screaming something about incest. She came back about two minutes later and threw a Dixie cup full of her own pee at Willy's head. Then she ran down the street. Willy grabbed me and twisted my arm till I said Cherri was sorry she did it. My arm was bruised for a week. Willy never said he was sorry. But that's because I was like a little sister.

Now I'm just Marty. On a day pass from the nuthouse.

The boat falls off the wind and slows. I look to the stern and Mrs. Fish waves. Willy gives me the finger behind his mother's back. Maybe I haven't lost my sister status completely. Except maybe with Cherri, who is still nowhere to be seen.

I lie back. Close my eyes and feel the sun bake into me. The boat rocks. I'm tired. So tired.

"Wake up, sleepyhead!"

I open my eyes a little. A black silhouette with a golden aura stands over me.

Oh, my God. I've died. And they actually let me into heaven.

214

"Come on, sit up," the angel says, and nudges me with her toe.

Angels don't nudge.

"What time is it?" I mumble.

"Lunchtime!" Cherri says, and whips something out from behind her back.

I rub my eyes. She is holding my favorite sandwich. Fried abalone.

"Don't tell me no!" she pleads.

"I was just –"

"Willy got up at 5:00 to go diving to get this for you and I've been slaving away down in the galley and you've got to eat this because your mom said they won't let you out again if you don't eat and I promised her you'd eat and . . ."

I can't concentrate on what she's saying. She is crushing the sandwich, waving it around. Red lips of tomato are flapping. An angry tongue of abalone sticks out at me. And mayonnaise spittle is flying everywhere. It looks like the sandwich is doing the talking.

". . . And I'm tired of this not-eating crap and what the hell are you staring at?"

"Cherri?"

"What?" she says, giving it a final shake.

"Can I have my lunch before you lose it overboard?"

"Ah . . . suuure. Sorry. It's a little wrecked."

"No, it's perfect."

Cherri pulls another sandwich from behind her.

"Do I have to eat that one too?"

"No, stupid. This one's for me. Can I sit with you, or do you want to eat . . . I mean be alone?"

"Stay. Please."

Cherri looks unsure.

"Don't worry. The only thing I'm going to bite is this sandwich."

We eat in silence. The sandwich tastes great. I try to take bigger bites and Cherri takes smaller ones so we are even. We never had to work at being friends before. Never had to think about it. But now I do. She is trying so hard and I've done nothing but kick dolphins and feel sorry for myself since I got on the boat. And Cherri's done nothing but think about me. I owe her an apology. For a lot of things.

"I'm sorry, Cherri."

"For what?" She smiles and drools mayonnaise.

"For being a pain in the ass."

"You've been sorry for a long time then."

I look over to see if she's kidding. She is. And I'm about to be serious. "I'm sorry about being with Paul."

Cherri stops chewing and swallows hard. "For the record, Zack and I were talking about you. We were worried. And as for Paul, it takes two to tango. Forget it. He wasn't worth losing you, my best friend."

"It's a lousy excuse, but I guess I needed someone to hang on to."

"You could've hung on to me."

"I didn't want to let you down."

"So you get together with my boyfriend?" Cherri says, and laughs.

I don't have an answer for that.

*

Lunch is over. Willy lets the sails fill again. We sit for a while.

Cherri clears her throat. Takes a deep breath and says, "I don't want you to fall . . . away."

"Fall away? Or fall apart?" It's a fair question.

"Both . . . I think we should stick together." I can see Cherri waiting for a sarcastic reply.

"Think you can handle being a rock?"

"Yeah . . . and you can be my barnacle."

A whistle breaks our Hallmark moment.

"I'M TACKING!"

"SHIT!"

I grab on to Cherri and we hit the deck together.

DAY 240
FEBRUARY 8

Sprout

"Can I speak to Judith White, please?" I whisper into the phone.

"Can I tell her who's calling, please?" the receptionist cans and pleases back.

It's always so tempting to just say no. "Tell her it's Marty."

"And your last name, please?"

"Black."

"And what company are you from?"

"I used to be with the Black and White Corporation, but they unincorporated."

"And who are you with now?"

"Myself."

"And the name of your organization?" the receptionist says, sounding as if she's smiling and congratulating herself on weeding out a call for her busy boss.

"Are you a receptionist or an antagonist?" *Or a former psych nurse.*

"I'm sorry?"

"How long have you been at your current position?"

"Six weeks. I apologize if I should know who you are."

Why should you know? I guess the boss doesn't brag about her kid anymore. "You can tell Judith *her daughter* is on the line." *Not to mention the edge.*

"Hold, please."

On to what?

I wait. I hold. On to the silence. While the receptionist talks to my mother, trying to explain why I might be angry and make it alright with my mom, who is probably trying to explain why she hadn't mentioned me in a way that would make it alright. I bet that the receptionist knew, by the end of her first day, that my mother needs things to be alright.

"Marty?"

"How did you know?" I kick the wall.

"Is anything wrong?" Mom's voice is tight.

"No."

"The new receptionist said you sounded upset."

Leave it, Marty. Bury it. Start over. "There is a garden here."

"It must be nice." Mom loosens up.

"Not really."

"Well . . ."

"But I want to do something about that."

"Like what?"

"Plant something."

"I could bring some plants. I can get them after work and bring them with me tonight."

"Thanks, Mom. But I would like to pick them out myself."

"Marty, you know you can't leave the unit again until you make your weight."

"I made it this morning – 118 pounds."

"That's terrific, honey! I'll bring some cham –"

"NO! You don't drink and I'm not ready to celebrate."

"Sorry, I meant nonalcoholic sparkling cider. Some responses are automatic."

"I'm sorry, Mom, I know." *I suffer from them too.* "But I don't want to talk about my weight. I'm trying to deal with it. By doing something positive. Can we go get something for the garden?" *Gaahd, I sound like a geek . . . at least I'm a positive geek.*

"It would be a lot easier if –"

"I know and I'm sorry to inconvenience you, but if you would take me to buy some seeds, I could plant them . . ."

"You want to plant seeds?"

"I . . . I want to start something from the beginning . . . and finish it."

"That sounds good."

"What grows really fast?"

Mom laughs.

"I remember when I was little and you taught kindergarten, or something. You used to bring home shoeboxes with things just sprouting."

"They were mostly marigolds and vegetables. The kids planted them from seeds and I'd bring them home to water over the weekend."

"Nobody here cares for marigolds." *They never cared for the last ones.* "What're the other easy ones to grow?"

"I'm not sure I remember, but I know radishes and carrots for sure."

"Carrots are perfect. Everybody likes carrots."

"I'll have the receptionist call around your area and find a good nursery."

"About the receptionist . . ."

"What's wrong with her?"

"Nothing. It was me. I was rude to her. Actually, I was more like a total asshole."

Mom starts laughing.

"Mom, will you tell her I'm sorry?"

Mom gets herself under control and says, "You can tell her yourself someday soon." She starts laughing again, but manages to choke out, "She said she couldn't wait to meet you."

DAY 241
FEBRUARY 9

Evacuation

Morning.

I work up gobs of saliva and hurl them into the sink. I keep going till there is nothing left but the elastic bands of spit hanging from my lips. I brush my teeth. Just in case. Because the bacteria in my mouth have been knitting sweaters all night for my molars. And those little sweaters are thick and heavy. I blow my nose. Think about pulling out the hairs inside it. Maybe pluck my eyebrows too. I sit on the toilet and pee hard and try to take a dump at the same time and roll my fists into my belly and press on all those organs. The bladder, the liver, the uterus, and my intestines. Anything that is attached to a hole I try to squish something out of. Out of every hole in your body you can pretty much get something. Even the wax on the end of the Q-tip, when you add it all up, equals a number. Some number that I won't have to look at when I step on the scale in five minutes.

I'm panicking.

I'm bound to hit some speed bumps on the road to recovery. I'm not a perfect nonanorexic yet. I'll confess later.

DAY 245
FEBRUARY 13

Last Supper

Everyone is inside the little cottage. I'm out by the bar-beque, thinking of what a beautiful day it is while I cook the cheeseburgers I picked for the Friday meal. They smell as good as I've always imagined.

I look through the window while I'm flipping the burgers. The new girl, who has been here four weeks, flips me the finger. She's not the only one. Everyone else is pissed at me too. About the french fries that Katherine is baking in the oven, and the Caesar salad with real bacon bits tossed by Mrs. Burns, and the fact that there are no carrots in sight.

Rhonda walks towards me from the main building. As she comes up beside me, she asks, "How are they coming?"

"Almost done."

"Good. Because it's time for you to be going."

"Going? . . . Going where?"

"Home."

"Today?"

"Right now. Nurse Brown is packing your things . . ."

"To make sure I don't steal any towels?"

". . . And your mom and Jackie are waiting for you in your room."

"You're kidding, right?"

"Nope."

"Do I get to say good-bye?" I look up and stare through the window.

"You said good-bye already. Little by little, as you got better. You don't belong with them anymore."

She's right. There is no room for tears in those tight faces. They'll just keep counting calories. Not the days till we meet again.

Katherine comes out of the cottage with a tray. "I'll take the burgers in, Marty. And you have a nice life," she says, and smiles.

"How did you know?"

"Mrs. Burns just told me."

"How?"

"She handed me a note in the kitchen. It said she saw *leaving* on Rhonda's face. The right kind of leaving."

I start laughing. "I can't believe this. Catwoman's passing notes and I'm being told I have to leave before I eat the burgers I've been dreaming about for three years."

Katherine grabs the spatula from me. "I'll take them inside."

"I feel sorry for you, Kath. They're going to be really mad about having to eat this meal without me, when it was my idea."

"Don't worry, I'll handle them." She piles up the burgers and takes them into the cottage kitchen. She puts the platter on the table. She turns to the window and winks. I wave.

I run to my garden. The little half-barrel in the concrete courtyard. I pull up the world's smallest carrot and walk to my room.

Rhonda, Jackie, Nurse Brown, and Mom are standing there talking. They stop as I pick up my bag with one hand. Dangle my carrot with the other.

"What's that? Jackie asks.

"Souvenir," I say, and grin.

Six Months Later . . .

AUGUST 13

"Can I have the rest of the afternoon off?" I say, and chug my carrot juice. For every free coffee Mrs. Van Daal gives me, she buys me a juice. And I drink it. Or I'm fired.

"You looking another job?" Mrs. Van Daal says, and puts down her tea.

"No."

"You should. At least you should be getting teaching about somesing besides soup and sandwiches. You can't vork here forever."

She must be psychic. I picked up the art school application yesterday. But I like it here. "I've only been back three months."

"Okay, you stay. For now."

"Thank you."

"You never ask time off before," Mrs. Van Daal says, and raises her eyebrows at me. "Somesing important, *klein muisje*?"

"I need to go see a friend."

Mrs. Van Daal pulls her chin in to her throat and raises her whole forehead this time. I know she will let me go, but not until I explain. I don't know if I can.

"I was in the hospital with her."

"Is she doing as good as you?"

"She's dead."

"You better go see her then."

I nod my head, but make no move to leave. We both sit in silence. The right kind of silence. The kind that gives you permission to come or go or cry.

"What is her favorite color?"

Or ask what a dead person's favorite color is – not was.

"Pink . . . but I don't think anyone knows that."

"I don't know your favorite color," she says, turning to me.

"It used to be black. But now I don't have one," I say, meeting her eyes.

I'm on the bus staring at the pink frosted cupcake Mrs. Van Daal gave me to take to Lily. When I said it was too late for her, Mrs. Van Daal said, "I know too late for Lily, but right time for you." And then she stuffed into my jacket pocket what I thought was some money to buy flowers.

I get off the bus and cross the street to catch a second bus. The bus arrives and I dig in my pocket for the transfer ticket. I hand it over and start to walk to the backseats.

The driver clears his throat and says, "Ah, miss? What am I supposed to do with this?"

I turn around and he's looking at me and holding up a newspaper clipping about the size of a transfer. I turn back, take it from him, and read: LOCAL WOMAN, SEVEN-TEEN YEARS OLD, ATTEMPTS SUICIDE BY OVERDOSE.

I put the cupcake on top of the bus fare box and the clipping in my mouth, and drive my hands into my pockets to find the transfer ticket. I'm shaking as I hand it to him. I sit down in the front seats behind the driver that are reserved for the handicapped because my legs are paralyzed.

I put Lily's cupcake beside me and try to hold still the clipping that Mrs. Van Daal gave me and that I tried to give to the bus driver. Even with two hands resting on my lap, it's hard to read: ATTEMPTS SUICIDE BY OVERDOSE. SHE WAS FOUND IN HER HOME AT APPROXIMATELY 7:00 P.M. LAST EVENING AND RUSHED TO A LOCAL HOSPI-TAL, WHERE SHE IS CURRENTLY IN A COMA AND LISTED IN CRITICAL CONDITION.

They didn't mention my name. But Mrs. Van Daal knew it was me. She cut it out of the police log in the paper and saved it. For over seven months.

For what?

I stare at the paper for a long time. And think about the space between swallowing those pills and reading about it in a piece of crumpled yellow newspaper. A lifetime.

Alivetime.

The trip to see Dad in New York. Looking at art and boats. Crossing a busy street on a red light, he held my hand and said, "It's alright, you're with me."

The grocery store with Mom. Laughing in the aisles about her allowing me three anorexic behaviors per trip. Our therapy sessions with Jackie. Finally letting out all the things I'd shoved down for so long. Going to lunch after because there was room for food. And Mom taking me to an AA meeting. Giving me credit for her quitting drinking. I said it was too much credit. She said, "You got me to stop. I have to stay sober."

And Cherri. Just being with Cherri.

The bus hits a bump.

I look out the window and see we are passing the cemetery. See all the graves of people who don't have to wait for buses, or worry about missing their stop. *Stop.*

"STOP!" I yell, and jump up next to the bus driver. "I'm sorry, this is where I need to get off."

The driver slows down. Looks in the side mirrors for cars and then looks in the rearview mirror at me and says, "I have a daughter. Same age as your friend – the one in your paper." He pulls the bus over and stops at the corner of the cemetery. "I guess she didn't make it," he says as he opens the doors.

I start down the steps, then turn around. He has sad eyes. I get to see a little of how I don't want to look to Lily.

"Actually she did. She's going to be okay," I say and step onto the sidewalk.

A little smile breaks into the corners of his eyes.

"She just needs a little work." I smile back.

"Don't we all," he says and laughs and closes the bus door.

A Little Time and a Taco

I realize that I don't know where Lily's grave is. And that I don't even know her last name. I go to the cemetery office. It's not hard to find – big gray building. Parked beside it are shiny black cars big enough to lie down in. No sun-roofs. Just curtains.

I walk to the front door, up a path bordered by new-looking granite headstones. No words on them. No heads under them. Showroom pieces. Last stop shopping.

The door is so heavy I grunt when I open it. My effort echoes through the foyer and brings clicking heels across the polished marble floor.

"Can I help you?" the woman with noisy shoes says in a quiet voice.

"I don't know where my friend is buried."

"Come with me and we'll figure that out," she says and turns for me to follow. Her heels sound like hammers and my running shoes squeak like rubber ducks.

She leads me to a little office. As soon as we pass through the doorway, all sound stops. Deep green carpet. A religious tapestry on one wall. Lined yellow drapes. Floral-patterned upholstered chairs. No rock anywhere. Only beautiful sound-sucking softness.

"I'm sorry for your loss," she says, looking into my eyes. "But I can help you find your friend's place of rest." She sits behind her desk and gestures for me to take a chair.

"Thank you."

"What is her name?"

"How did you know?"

She points to the melting pink cupcake. "I didn't think you came here for a picnic."

"No. It's for Lily."

She types into her computer. "And Lily's last name?"

"I don't know." I look down at my lap.

"Do you know when she passed away?"

"Not exactly . . . Christmas." *I wasn't around. Wasn't around when she needed me. Want to leave now. Want this woman to stop asking me what I know and start judging me for what I don't.*

I get up from the chair.

"When was Lily born?"

"Today. Nine years ago," I say, and sink back into the chair. A box of Kleenex slides onto my lap. The sight of it makes my eyes hot and my throat close up. My nose starts to run. I sneeze.

"You're not allergic to dogs are you?" She frowns.

I shake my head *no*. It's a strange question because I saw a sign saying NO DOGS ALLOWED when I came in the front gate.

"Good," she says and smiles.

Someone told me once that every time a person sneezes, someone dies. I guess I just brought them more business.

I sneeze again, trying to hold back my tears. I hear a shuffling sound.

She opens a drawer in her desk, looks into it, and says, "You can come out now. It's okay. Go do your job."

From behind the desk trots a dog smaller than the box of tissues on my lap. It's a Chihuahua. It sits at my feet and looks up at me with big brown bulging eyes, like marbles in a white cue ball of a head. It yips a warning before launching itself onto the arm of my chair. It looks at me, then at the tissues, then back to me again.

"His name is Taco."

Taco flattens his ears, pulls his dog lips back into a smile, licks his nose with a little pink Band-Aid of a tongue, and wags his tail along the chair arm like a windshield wiper.

I pat my lap. He steps onto it and starts licking my hand.

Lily would have loved you.

I cry now. Right in front of this patient stranger and silly dog. I can't help it.

"Good boy, Taco. Go to work," she says and leaves the office.

Taco starts nudging the box on my lap. I grab it so it doesn't fall. He sticks his face into the box and scoops tissues out with his nose. He grips one with his teeth and waves it around like a bullfighter with his cape. He stops and stares at me. Drops the Kleenex and snatches another one and flings it at me. I am trying to cry for Lily and not for me, and not laugh at this dog who is just doing his job. He is a canine Kleenex dispenser. And he is going to bury me if I can't find his OFF switch.

"Taco, if I take one, I won't be able to stop."

Taco stops his frenzy. Sits on my thigh, narrows his eyes, and growls.

I take a tissue. Taco curls into a ball like a cat and goes to sleep.

I cry and laugh and cry until I use up all the Kleenexes that Taco has prescribed.

Taco's boss comes back. She sits behind her desk. "I hope you don't mind that I left. I thought you could use a little time . . . and a Taco." She smiles.

She's not talking about food, Marty. Just treating you like a normal person. Get used to it.

"It's a little inside joke around here. Whenever someone is sad, we say they could use a Taco."

"He must be a busy dog in a place like this."

"He certainly earns his keep. We don't allow dogs here, but two years ago he ran away from a funeral and into the bottom drawer of my desk. The old man who was his best friend is buried under there," she says, pointing to a tree about forty feet from her window. "When I found Taco, I called the relatives but nobody wanted him. He looked so small and sad and scared that I started to cry. He handed me a tissue and I hired him."

I stroke Taco, who is sleeping on the job.

She leans across her desk and talks to the lump of warm dough, rising and falling in my lap. "Okay, Taco, pick up. Good boy."

Taco stands, stretches, and takes a little snaky lick of Lily's cupcake. He picks up Kleenexes from my hand and jumps down to get those that have fallen on the floor. He drops them in the wastepaper basket and disappears around the desk. He gives one sharp bark and scratches at the drawer. The woman opens it and I hear Taco jump in.

She unfolds a pamphlet and pushes it across her desk at me. "Lily is buried in section 32. I've drawn a yellow line to show you how to get there." She clears her throat and says, "I assume you didn't know Lily for long since you don't know her last name. Something about Lily's gravesite struck me as odd, so I did a little digging – sorry, I didn't mean it that way. What I'm saying is, Lily's site was purchased almost nine years ago.

"You look upset. I'm sorry. When a child dies, it's always a tragedy. A tragedy that many people who were close to the child never recover from. I would guess that when Lily was born, something was so wrong that they thought she wouldn't live."

"She had a heart condition. I didn't know until after."

"And if she'd wanted you to know, she would have told you. Maybe to you she wanted to be *just Lily*."

"Maybe."

"And knowing that she might die, you can only hope she led a full life."

"Mostly she ran on empty. But I hope she's making up for it."

Lily's Grave

Section 32.

I head for a big cross on an ominous monument. *Knowing Lily's parents*. The gravesite is immaculate. Well watered and not a blade of grass any higher than its neighbor, like it was clipped with manicure scissors. And it has a tin cup in the middle. Like a putting green with flowers instead of a flag. It's not Lily's. It's some guy's named Fred.

233

I almost miss her grave. Because it's not the way I imagined.

It's the way I imagined mine.

Gravestone – black granite. Untidy. Wild roses – pink. Blooms, big and flat like the palm of a hand. Open, so you can see the parts the closefisted roses always hide.

Dandelions stand in the tall grass, like children looking up at their relatives.

Even lilies. With the flowers gone. Only the stems to remind me that they were there at all.

I would love a grave like this. Except for the name . . .

LILY HILLS

And the date . . .

DIED – TOO SOON